Kristy and the Mother's Day Surprise

THE BABY-SITTERS CLUB®

Kristy and the Mother's Day Surprise

ANN M. MARTIN

SCHOLASTIC INC.

For Amy Berkower

Copyright © 1989 by Ann M. Martin

This book was originally published in paperback by Scholastic Inc. in 1989.

ISBN 978-1-338-81503-0

10 9 8 7 6 5 4 3 2 1   23 24 25 26 27

Printed in the U.S.A. 40
This edition first printing 2023

Book design by Maeve Norton

CHAPTER 1

I've been thinking about families lately, wondering what makes one. Is a family really a mother, a father, and a kid or two? I hope not, because if that's a family, then I haven't got one. And neither do a lot of other people I know. For instance, Nannie, Mom's mother, lives all by herself. But I still think of her as a family — a one-person family. And I think of my own family as a real family . . . I guess.

What I mean is, well, my family didn't start out the way it is now. It started out as two families that split up and came together as . . . Uh-oh. I know that's confusing. I'm a little ahead of myself. I better back up and begin at the beginning.

This is the beginning: Hi! I'm Kristy Thomas. I'm thirteen years old. I'm in eighth grade. I'm the president of the Baby-sitters Club (more about that later). I like sports, and I guess you could say I'm a tomboy. (Well, wouldn't you be one if you had a whole bunch of brothers?) I'm not the neatest person in the world. I don't care much about boys or clothes. I'm famous for coming up with big ideas.

Okay, enough about me. Let me tell you about —

Knock, knock.

Darn, I thought. Who could that be? It was a Friday evening and I didn't have any plans or even a baby-sitting job. I was in my bedroom, just messing around, enjoying my free time.

"Who's there?" I called.

"Oswald!" my little sister replied.

Oswald? *Oh. . . .* "Oswald who?" I asked.

"Help! Help! Oswald my gum!"

I was laughing as I opened the door and found a very giggly Karen in the hallway.

"Pretty funny," I said, as Karen ran into my room and threw herself on my bed. "Where'd you hear that one?"

"In school. Nancy told it to me. What are you doing with the door closed?"

"Just fooling around."

"But this is our first night here."

"I'm sorry, Karen. I didn't mean to shut you out. It's just that I had a rotten week at school and today was especially rotten, so I wanted to be by myself for awhile."

You're probably wondering why Karen said, "But this is our first night here." I think now would be a good time to explain my family to you. See, Karen isn't exactly my sister. She's my stepsister. Her little brother Andrew is my stepbrother, and her father is my stepfather. Karen and Andrew only live with us part-time. I like when they come over because then my family consists of Mom, Watson (he's my stepfather), Sam, Charlie, and David Michael (they're my brothers), and Karen and Andrew. Oh, and Shannon and Boo-Boo. They're our dog and cat, and they're part of the family, too.

How did I get this weird family? Well, you can probably imagine. My mom and dad were divorced. They got divorced right after David Michael was born. Then, a couple of years ago, Mom met Watson and started going out with him. Watson was divorced, too. And after awhile, Mom and Watson got married, and then Mom and my brothers and I moved into Watson's house. That's how I got my big family. The only unusual thing is that Watson is a millionaire. Honest. That's why we moved into his house. It's a lot bigger than our old one. It's huge. In fact, it's basically a mansion. Living in a mansion here in Stoneybrook, Connecticut, is fun, but sometimes I miss my old house. It's on the other side of town, where all my friends are.

So now I'm part of a six-kid family. My brother Charlie is the oldest kid. He's seventeen, a senior in high school, and thinks he's a big shot. Sam is fifteen. He's a sophomore in high school. Then there's me, then David Michael, who's seven, and then Karen and Andrew, who are six and four. Usually, Karen and Andrew only live with us every other weekend and for two weeks during the summer. The rest of the time they live with their mother, who's not too far away — in a different neighborhood in Stoneybrook. But the night Karen bounced into my room with her knock-knock joke was the beginning of a much longer stay. Karen and Andrew were going to be with us for several weeks while their mother and stepfather went on a business trip.

"Knock, knock," said Karen again.

"Who's there?" I replied.

"Hey, Karen! Come here!" It was David Michael, yelling down the hall.

"What?" Karen yelled back.

"Come look at this bug!" (David Michael just loves bugs.)

Karen was off my bed and out of my room in a flash.

I smiled. I really like my family, especially when Karen and Andrew are here. The bigger, the better. Sometimes I think of my friends as family, too. Is that weird? I don't know. But my friends do feel like family. I guess I'm mostly talking about my friends in the Baby-sitters Club. That's a club I started myself. Actually, it's more of a business. My friends and I sit for families in Stoneybrook and we earn a lot of money.

Here's who's in the club: me, Claudia Kishi, Mary Anne Spier, Dawn Schafer, Mallory Pike, and Jessi Ramsey. We are six very different people, but we get along really well (most of the time). That's the way it is with families.

For instance, I'm pretty outgoing (some people say I have a big mouth), and as I mentioned before, I like sports and couldn't care less about clothes or boys. My best friend is Mary Anne Spier (she's our club secretary) and we are *so* different. Mary Anne is quiet and shy, hates sports, is becoming interested in clothes, has a boyfriend, and comes from a very small family. She lives with just her dad and her kitten, Tigger. Her mom died a long time ago. Mary Anne and I have always been different and have always been best friends. We lived next door to each other until Mom married Watson, so we practically grew up together. One thing that's the same about us is our looks. We both have brown hair and brown eyes and are short for our age.

The vice-president of the Baby-sitters Club is Claudia Kishi. Claud lives across the street from Mary Anne. There is nothing, and I mean *nothing*, typical or average or ordinary about Claudia. To begin with, she's Japanese American. Her hair is silky and long and jet-black. Her eyes are dark. And her skin, well, I wish it were mine. I'm sure her skin doesn't even know what a pimple is. Which is interesting when you consider Claudia's eating habits. Claud is pretty much addicted to junk food. Her parents don't like her to eat much of it, though, so she has to resort to hiding it in her room. Everywhere you look, you find something: a package of red-hots in the pencil cup, a bag of Cheese Doodles under her bed, a box of Cracker Jacks in the closet. This makes for a crowded room because Claudia is a pack rat. She has to be. She's an artist and needs to collect things for her work, such as shells, leaves, and interesting pebbles. Plus, she has tons of supplies — paper, canvases, paints, pastels, charcoals — and most of them are stored under her bed. Claud likes Nancy Drew mysteries and is a terrible student (even though she's smart). She lives with her parents, her grandmother, Mimi, and her older sister, Janine. It's too bad that Claud is such a poor student, because Janine is a genius. One last thing about Claudia — her clothes. They are just . . . so cool. Well, I mean Claud is. She's the coolest kid in our grade. Her clothes are wild. Claud loves trying new things and she has an incredible imagination. She wears hats, weird jewelry (she makes some of it), bright colors — anything she can get away with!

Dawn Schafer is the club's treasurer. Now *she's* got an interesting family. Dawn used to live in California. She lived there with her parents and Jeff, her younger brother. Then her parents got divorced and Mrs. Schafer moved Dawn and Jeff all the way across country to Stoneybrook. The reason she chose Stoneybrook is she grew up here, and her parents (Dawn's grandparents) still live here. We got to know Dawn and she joined the Baby-sitters Club and everything seemed great. Except that Jeff missed his father and California — a lot. Finally, he moved back there. Now Dawn's family is split in half and separated by a continent. Dawn seems to be handling the changes well, though. She's pretty mature. And she's a real individual. She solves her own problems, makes her own decisions, and isn't too affected by what other people think of her or tell her. Plus, Dawn is neat and organized, which makes her a good treasurer. Although Dawn has been living in Connecticut for over a year now, she still looks sort of Californian. She's got long hair that is the blondest I've ever seen. It's almost white. And her eyes are sparkly and pale blue. In the summer she gets this amazing tan. (The rest of the year she just has freckles.) And her clothes are casual and as individualistic as she is. She likes to wear layers of things — a short tank top over a long tank top, or socks over tights. Dawn is pretty cool.

The two junior members of our club are Jessi Ramsey and Mallory Pike. They're junior members because they're younger than the rest of us eighth-graders. Mal and Jessi are in sixth grade. They haven't been club members as long as us older girls. Still, they're beginning to feel like family to me.

Mallory used to be someone our club sat *for*. Isn't that weird? Now she's a sitter herself. Mal is the oldest of eight kids. (Talk about big families.) The Baby-sitters Club still takes care of her younger brothers and sisters pretty often.

Anyway, Mal is a great sitter. She's levelheaded and responsible — good in an emergency. And she's the most practical person I know. Mal is struggling to grow up. Being eleven can be very difficult, and Mal thinks her parents treat her like a baby. However, they're starting to let up. Recently, they allowed Mal to get her ears pierced and her hair cut. (She had to get braces, too, though, and her parents said she's too young for contact lenses.) Mal likes reading (especially books about horses), writing, and drawing. She thinks she might want to be an author of children's books when she grows up.

Jessi (short for Jessica) Ramsey is Mal's best friend. Like Dawn, she's a newcomer to Stoneybrook, Connecticut. In fact, she's a newer newcomer than Dawn is. Her family moved here from New Jersey at the beginning of the school year. They moved because Mr. Ramsey changed jobs. In many ways, Jessi and Mal are alike. Jessi also loves to read, she wears glasses (just for reading), and she thinks *her* parents treat her like a baby, although they did let her get her ears pierced when Mal had hers done. But there are some big differences between Jessi and Mal. I guess the biggest is that Jessi is Black and Mal is white. This hasn't made a bit of difference to the girls, but the

9

Ramseys sure had some trouble when they first moved here. Not many Black families live in Stoneybrook, and some people gave the Ramseys a hard time. Jessi says things are settling down, though. Another difference between Mal and Jessi is that Mal likes to write and Jessi likes to dance. Jessi is a ballerina. She's very talented. I've seen her dance — *on stage*. I was really impressed. The third difference is that Mal's family is huge, while Jessi's is average — Jessi; her parents; her younger sister, Becca; and her baby brother, Squirt.

And that's it. Those are the people in my family. It's a big family, when you add the members of the Baby-sitters Club. I could add a few more, too, I thought later that night as I lay in bed. There's Nannie. There's Stacey McGill, who used to be a member of the club, but who had to move to New York City. There are Shannon and Logan, whom I'll tell you about later. And there's my real father. . . . But, no, he doesn't count. Somebody who never writes, never calls, never remembers your birthday, never says he loves you, doesn't count at all.

I was growing sleepy, and I forgot about my father. Instead, I thought of my gigantic family. I fell asleep smiling.

CHAPTER 2

As president of the Baby-sitters Club, I get to run the meetings. I adore being in charge. Club meetings are the best times of my week.

"Order! Order, you guys!" I said.

It was Monday afternoon at five-thirty, time for our meeting to begin. Everyone had arrived and was sitting (or sprawling) in her usual place. As president, I always sit in the director's chair and wear my visor. I stick a pencil over my ear. That way, I *look* like I'm in charge. Claudia, Dawn, and Mary Anne loll around on the bed, and Jessi and Mal sit on the floor.

We hold our meetings in Claudia's room. She has her own phone.

This is how our club works: Three times a week, on Mondays, Wednesdays, and Fridays from five-thirty until six, our club meets in Claudia's bedroom. People who need sitters call us during our meetings. They're practically guaranteed a sitter. With six club members, one of us is bound to be free. So we wind up with lots of jobs. Pretty neat, huh?

The idea for the club was mine. (That's how I got to be the president.) It came to me way back at the beginning of seventh grade, before Mom was really thinking about marrying Watson. We still lived in this neighborhood then. In fact, we lived right across the street from Claudia. Anyway, one day Mom needed a sitter for David Michael, who had just turned six. I wasn't free and neither was Sam nor Charlie. So Mom got on the phone and began making call after call, trying to find a sitter. I felt bad for my mother, and even worse for David Michael, who was watching everything. And that was when I got my great idea. Wouldn't it be wonderful if Mom could make just one call and reach a whole bunch of baby-sitters at once? She'd find a sitter much faster that way.

So I got together with Mary Anne and Claudia and told them about my idea. We decided to form the Baby-sitters Club. We also decided we'd need more than three members, so we asked Stacey McGill, a new friend of Claudia's, to join the club, too. Stacey had just moved to Stoneybrook from New York City because her father's job had changed. I could see right away why she and Claudia had become friends so fast. Stacey awed Mary Anne and me. She seemed years older than twelve — very sophisticated with trendy clothes, pierced ears, and permed hair. But she was also very nice. Furthermore, she'd had plenty of baby-sitting experience in New York, so we knew she'd be a good addition to the club.

After Stacey agreed to join us, we sent around flyers and ran an ad in Stoneybrook's newspaper so people would know when to call us — and we were in business! The club was great. By the time Dawn moved to town, we needed another sitter, and later, when Stacey moved back to New York, we were doing so much business that we replaced her with both Jessi and Mal. And somewhere along the line we decided that we better have a couple of people lined up whom we could call on in case *none* of us could take a job. So we signed up two associate members, Shannon Kilbourne and Logan Bruno. Shannon lives across the street from me in my new neighborhood. We're friends, sort of. Logan is a *boy* — and he's Mary Anne's boyfriend! Shannon and Logan don't come to the meetings. We just call them when we need them, so that we don't have to disappoint any of our clients by saying that no sitters are available.

I run our meetings in the most businesslike way I can. As president, that's my job. Also, I come up with ideas for the club and generally just try to keep things going smoothly.

The job of the vice-president is, well . . . To be honest, Claudia Kishi is the vice-president because she has her own phone and personal, private phone number. The club uses her phone so we don't have to tie up some grownup's phone three times a week. The only thing is, our clients sometimes forget when our meetings are and call at other times. Claudia has to deal with those job offers, and she handles things really well.

Mary Anne Spier, our secretary, has the biggest job of any of us. Our club has a notebook (I'll tell you about that soon) and a record book. Mary Anne is the one who keeps the record book in order and up-to-date. She writes down our clients' names, addresses, and phone numbers and is responsible for scheduling *all* our sitting jobs on the appointment pages. This is more difficult than it sounds, since she has to keep track of things like Jessi's ballet classes, Claud's art lessons, Mal's orthodontist appointments, and you name it. I don't think Mary Anne has ever made a mistake, though.

Our treasurer, Dawn Schafer, collects dues from us every Monday and keeps track of the money that's in our treasury. We use the money for three things. One, to pay Charlie to drive me to and from the meetings, since I live so far from Claudia now. Two, for club parties and sleepovers. Every now and then we like to give ourselves a treat. Three, to buy materials for Kid-Kits. What are Kid-Kits? Well, they're one of my ideas. A Kid-Kit is a box that we fill with our old toys, books, and games, and also some new things, like coloring books, crayons, or sticker books. Each of us has her own Kid-Kit, and we need money to replace the things that get used up. The children we sit for love the Kid-Kits. Bringing one along on a job is like bringing a toy store. It makes the kids happy. And when the kids are happy, their parents are happy. . . . And when their parents are happy, they call the Baby-sitters Club again!

Mallory and Jessi, our junior officers, don't have any special jobs. The junior officers simply aren't allowed to sit at night unless they're sitting for their own brothers and sisters, so when Mary Anne schedules jobs, she tries to give the after-school and weekend jobs to Jessi and Mallory first. That way the rest of us will be free to take the evening jobs.

And that's it. That's how our club — Oh, wait. One more thing. The club notebook. The notebook is different from the record book, but just as important. It's more of a diary than a notebook. Any time one of us club members goes on a baby-sitting job, she's responsible for writing up the job in the notebook. Then, once a week, each of us is supposed to read the notebook. This is really very helpful. We learn how our friends solve sitting problems, or if a kid that we're going to be taking care of has a new fear, a new hobby, etc. Some of the girls think that writing in the notebook is a boring chore, but I think it's valuable.

Okay. That really *is* it. Now you know how our club began and how it runs, so let's get back to business.

After I had said "Order!" for about the third time, everyone settled down. "Any business?" I asked.

"Dues day!" announced Dawn. She bounced off the bed, blonde hair flying. The treasury envelope was in her hands, and she opened it.

"*Oh,*" groaned the rest of us. We earn a lot of money baby-sitting, but we don't like to part with it for dues, even though we know we have to.

"Aw, come on," said Dawn. "It isn't that bad. Besides, think of me. I have to listen to this moaning and complaining every Monday afternoon." Dawn collected the money, then handed some of it to me. "That's for Charlie," she said. "We have to pay him today."

I nodded. "Thanks, Dawn."

My friends settled down. Claudia leaned against one of her pillows and began braiding her hair. Mary Anne unwrapped a piece of gum. Dawn flipped through the pages of the notebook. On the floor, Mallory doodled in one of Claudia's sketchbooks, and Jessi absentmindedly lifted the cover of a shoe box labeled PASTILS AND CHARCAOLS (Claudia isn't a great speller), and exclaimed, "Hey, there's M and M's in here!"

"Oh, yeah," replied Claud. "I forgot about those. Hand them around, Jessi, okay?"

"Sure!" said Jessi. She took out the bag of candy, replaced the lid on the box, opened the bag, and sent it around Claud's bedroom.

Everyone took a handful of M&M's except for Dawn, who mostly eats health food — she won't even eat meat — and can't stand junk food, especially candy. Claudia remembered this and handed Dawn a package of whole-wheat crackers. Dawn looked really grateful.

This is just one of the things I love about my club family. We really care about each other. We look out for each other and do nice things for each other. Of course, we fight, too — we've had some whoppers — but that's part of being a family.

"Well, any more club business?" I asked.

Nobody answered.

"Okay, then. We'll just wait for the phone to ring." I picked up the record book and began looking at the appointment calendar. "Gosh," I said, "I cannot believe it's already April. Where did the school year go? It feels like it was just September."

"I know," agreed Mary Anne. "Two more months and school will be over." She looked pretty pleased.

"Yeah," said Dawn happily. "Summer. Hot weather. I'll get to visit Dad and Jeff in California again."

"Whoa!" I cried. I was still looking at our calendar. "Guess what. I just realized that Mother's Day is coming up — soon. It's in less than three weeks."

"Oh, brother. Gift time," murmured Mallory. "I *never* know what to get Mom. None of us does. She always ends up with a bunch of stuff she doesn't want and doesn't know what to do with. Like every year, Margo" (Margo is Mal's seven-year-old sister) "makes her a handprint in clay and paints it green. What's Mom going to do with all those green hand sculptures? And the triplets" (ten-year-old boys) "always go to the dime store and get her really ugly plastic earrings or a horrible necklace or something."

"Once," said Jessi, "my sister gave our mother a bag of chocolate kisses and then ate them herself."

We began to laugh.

"This year," Claud began, "I am going to give my mother the perfect present."

"What?" I asked.

Claud shrugged. "I don't know yet."

"I never have to think of Mother's Day presents," said Mary Anne softly.

The talking and laughing stopped. How is it that I forget about Mary Anne's problem year after year? I never remember until somebody, usually the art teacher, is saying something like, "All right, let's begin our Mother's Day cards," or "I know your mothers will just love these glass mosaics." Then I watch Mary Anne sink lower and lower in her seat. Why don't the teachers say, "If you want to make a Mother's Day gift, come over here. The rest of you may read." Or something like that. It would be a lot easier on the kids who don't need to make Mother's Day stuff.

Dawn looked at Mary Anne and awkwardly patted her shoulder.

Claud said, "Sorry, Mary Anne."

We feel bad for her but we don't quite know what to say. Sorry your mother died? Sorry the greeting card people invented Mother's Day and you have to feel bad once a year? Sorry we have moms and you don't?

I was relieved when the telephone rang. (We all were.) It gave us something to do. I answered the phone, and Mary Anne took over the record book.

"Hi, Mrs. Newton," I said. "Friday afternoon? ... Yeah, it is short notice, I guess, but I'll check. I'll get right back to you." I hung up. "Check Friday after school," I told Mary Anne. "This Friday."

Mary Anne checked. "Claudia's free," she said. "She's the only one."

I glanced at Claud and she nodded.

So I called Mrs. Newton back. "Claudia will be there," I told her. We said good-bye and hung up. The Newtons are some of our oldest clients. They have two kids — Jamie, who's four, and

20

Lucy, who's just a baby. We all love sitting at the Newtons', but Claudia especially loves it. I knew she was happy with her job.

The phone rang several more times after that. All job calls. Then, toward the end of the meeting, we began talking about Mother's Day again. We couldn't help it. We knew Mary Anne felt sad, but the rest of us really needed to think about what to give our moms.

"Flowers?" suggested Jessi.

We shook our heads.

"Chocolate-covered cherries?" suggested Claudia.

We shook our heads.

"Oh, well. It's six o'clock," I announced. "Meeting's over. Don't worry — we have plenty of time to think of presents. See you guys in school tomorrow."

CHAPTER 3

When I left Claudia's house, Charlie was waiting for me in the Kishis' driveway. He has been really good about remembering to drive me to and from the meetings of the Baby-sitters Club. We *are* paying him, but still . . . I keep thinking he might get tied up with an after-school activity and forget me sometime.

Moving across town was *so* inconvenient. I'm not near any of my closest friends, and I'm not near my school. Now I have to get rides all the time and take the bus to school. The other kids in my new neighborhood go to private schools. But I wanted to stick with my regular school (so did my brothers), so we're the only ones who go to public. We really stand out.

Charlie pulled into the drive, and Watson's huge house (well, *our* huge house) spread before us. I am amazed every time I see it. We parked, and my brother and I went inside.

We were greeted by Sam. "Boy, Kristy. I don't know how you do it," was the first thing he said.

"Do what?"

"Baby-sit so much without going looney tunes."

I grinned. Sam had been watching David Michael, Andrew, and Karen, since Mom and Watson were still at work. "Baby-sitting is easy," I replied. "It's a piece of cake. What happened?"

"What do you mean 'What happened?' Nothing *happened*. They're just kids. I'm worn out. I couldn't give another cannonball ride if my life depended on it."

"That's Charlie's fault for inventing cannonballs," I told Sam.

At that moment, Andrew came barreling into the front hall, crying, "Sam! Sam! I need a cannonball ride!"

Without pausing, Sam picked Andrew up, Andrew curled himself into a ball, and Sam charged off toward the kitchen, shouting, "Ba-boom-ba-boom-ba-boom-ba-boom."

"I thought he couldn't give another cannonball ride," said Charlie.

"Andrew is hard to resist," I told him.

Dinner that night was noisy. It was one of the few times when everyone was home. Andrew and Karen usually aren't with us, and when they are, they're almost always here on a weekend — when Charlie's out on a date or Sam is at a game at school, or *something*. But that night was different. We ate in the dining room. Watson sat at one end of the table, Mom at the other. David Michael, Karen, and I sat along one side of the table; Charlie, Sam, and Andrew sat across from us.

When everyone had been served, Mom said, "Isn't this nice?" She had been a little emotional lately.

"It's terrific," agreed Watson, who sounded *too* enthusiastic.

Mom and Watson get all worked up whenever we're together as a family, and I know why. I like my family and everything. I like us a lot. But sometimes I think we feel more like pieces of a family instead of a whole family. We're a shirt whose seams haven't all been stitched up. I mean, Mom and Watson got married, but I would only go to Mom if I needed to borrow money. And Andrew usually heads for Watson if he's hurt himself or doesn't feel well. *We're* Mom's kids and *they're* Watson's kids. Two teams on the same playing field.

Don't get me wrong. It isn't bad. Really. Our family just needs to grow together — so Mom and Watson make a huge deal out of things like all of us sitting down at the dinner table.

Our dinners are usually not very quiet. That night, David Michael started things off by singing softly, *"They built the ship* Titanic *to sail the ocean blue. A sadder ship the waters never knew. She was on her maiden trip when an iceboard hit the ship —"*

"Cut it *out*!" cried Karen suddenly. "I hate that song. All the people die. Besides, it's 'ice*berg*,' not 'ice*board*.'"

"I know that," said David Michael. But he didn't. He had said 'iceboard' every time he had sung that song.

He stopped singing. He made a rhythm band out of his plate, glass, fork, and spoon.

Andrew joined him.

Chink-a-chink. Chinkety-chink, chink.

Mom beamed. Why did she look so happy? Usually dinnertime rhythm bands gave her a headache.

"Hey, Karen. Your epidermis is showing," said Sam from across the table.

"What? What?" Karen, flustered, began checking her clothes. Finally, she said haughtily, "Sam. I am not wearing a dress. How can my epipotomus be showing?"

We couldn't help it. Watson, Mom, Charlie, Sam, David Michael, and I began to laugh. Not rudely, just gently. Well, all right. David Michael laughed rudely — loudly, anyway.

"What?" Karen demanded.

"It's 'epidermis,' not 'epipotomus,' " said David Michael, glad to be able to correct *her*, "and it means 'skin.' "

Karen looked questioningly at Sam.

"He's right," said Sam. "It does mean 'skin.' "

"My *skin* is showing?" said Karen. "Oh, my *skin* is showing! That's funny! I'm going to say that to everyone in my class tomorrow."

"Now let's have a little eating," said Watson.

For a few moments, we ate. I was working on a mouthful of lima beans when I heard David Michael murmur, *"Beans, beans, they're good for your heart. The more you eat, the more —"*

I kicked him under the table. Not hard. Just enough to make him stop. Mom and Watson *hate* that song.

But soon my brother was singing, *"Beans, beans, the magical fruit. The more you eat —"*

I kicked him again. "Cut it *out.*"

"It's a different song."

"Not different enough."

David Michael grew silent.

At her end of the table, Mom put down her fork and looked lovingly at Watson. "We're so lucky," she said.

Watson smiled.

I glanced at Sam and Charlie. Mom had been acting weird lately.

"We've got six beautiful children —"

"I am not beautiful," said David Michael. "I'm a boy."

"We live in a lovely town," continued Mom, "we like our jobs, we have a gorgeous house . . . with plenty of rooms. Do you realize that we have three spare bedrooms?"

My mother was looking at us kids.

I glanced at Sam and Charlie again. They shrugged.

"It *is* a nice house, Mom," I agreed.

Mom nodded. "Plenty of extra space."

Suddenly Sam said, "Hey, Mom, you're not pregnant, are you?"

(My mother *could* have been pregnant. She's only in her late thirties. She had Charlie right after she graduated from college.)

"No," Mom replied. "I'm not. . . . But how would you kids feel about another brother or sister?"

Oh. So she was trying to *become* pregnant.

"Another brother or sister?" David Michael repeated dubiously.

"A *baby*?" squeaked Andrew and Karen.

"Great!" said Sam and Charlie.

"Terrific!" I added honestly. I love babies. Imagine having one right in my house, twenty-four hours a day.

But the little kids just couldn't be enthusiastic.

"Why do you want a baby?" asked Karen bluntly.

"Oh, we didn't say we want a *baby* —" Watson began.

But before he could finish, Andrew spoke up. "A baby," he said, "would be the youngest person in the family. But that's *me. I'm* the youngest. I don't want a baby."

"Babies smell," added Karen.

"They cry," said David Michael. "And burp and spit up and get baby food in their hair. And you have to *change their diapers.*"

"Kids, kids," exclaimed Watson, holding his hands up. "Elizabeth just asked about another brother or sister, that's all."

Silence.

At last David Michael said, "Well, brothers and sisters start out as babies, don't they?"

And Andrew said, "I think we've got enough kids around here."

"Yeah," agreed Karen and David Michael.

But I couldn't help saying, "Another kid would be great. Really."

Sam and Charlie nodded.

No one seemed to know what to say then, but it didn't matter because Boo-Boo came into the dining room carrying a mole he'd caught, and we all jumped out of our chairs. The poor mole was still alive, so we had to get it away from Boo-Boo and then put it back outside where it belonged.

That was the end of dinner.

Later that night, I lay in bed, thinking. Sometimes I get in bed early just so I can do that. First I thought about Boo-Boo and the mole. Charlie and I had caught Boo-Boo and held him. And David Michael had gotten Boo-Boo to open his mouth, which had caused the mole to drop out and land in the oven mitts Mom was wearing. Then Mom, Karen, Andrew, and David Michael had taken the mole into the backyard and let it loose in some shrubbery. It had scampered off.

I thought of Mom wanting to have another baby. Even though she's kind of old for that, it made sense. I mean, she's married to Watson now, so I guessed that she and Watson wanted a baby of their own. Boy. Mom would have five kids and two stepkids then.

She would need an extra special Mother's Day present. What on earth could I give her? I slid over in bed so I could see the moon out my window.

The moon was pretty, but it was no help.

Jewelry? Nah. Mom likes to choose her own. Stockings? Boring. Candy or flowers? Let Watson do that. Something for her desk at the office? Maybe. Clothes? If I could afford anything.

I had a feeling I was missing the point, though. I wanted to say thank you to Mom for being such a wonderful mother. (She really is.) So I needed to give her something special, something that would tell her, "You're the best mom. Thanks." But what would say that?

I thought and thought. And then it came to me. It was another one of my ideas. Carrying it off might take some work, but my friends and I could do it.

I couldn't wait until the next meeting of the Baby-sitters Club.

CHAPTER 4

I don't know whether to describe myself as a patient person or not. I mean, when I'm baby-sitting, I can sit for fifteen minutes, waiting for a four-year-old who wants to tie his own shoelaces. But when I have a big idea, I want to get on with it right away. And I had a *huge* idea.

On Wednesday, I begged Charlie to leave early for the club meeting. I reached Claudia's at 5:15.

None of my friends was there, not even Claudia.

"She is baby-sitting," Mimi told me. "At Marshalls'. Back at . . . at five, no at thirty-five. No, um . . . back for meeting."

Mimi is Claudia's grandmother, and we all love her. She had a stroke last summer and it affected her speech. Also, she is getting a little slower, and . . . I don't know. She just seems older. I wish people didn't have to change.

But they do.

"Go on upstairs?" Mimi said to me, as if it were a question.

"Is that okay?" I replied.

Mimi nodded, so I kissed her cheek and ran to Claud's room. I found the notebook and record book and set them on the bed. Then I put on my visor. I stuck a pencil over my ear and sat in the director's chair. I was ready for the meeting. The only thing I needed was all the rest of the club members.

Claudia arrived first. The others trickled in after her. By 5:29, the six of us had gathered. I was so excited that I rushed through our opening business and then exclaimed, "I've got an idea!"

"This sounds like a big one," said Dawn.

"It's pretty big," I agreed.

"Bigger than the Kid-Kits?" Mary Anne wanted to know.

"Much."

"Bigger than the *club*?" asked Mallory, awed.

"Not quite. This is it: I was trying to come up with a Mother's Day present for my mom," I began. (I couldn't look at Mary Anne while I talked about Mother's Day. I just couldn't.) "And I was thinking that her present should be really special. That it should have something to do with saying thank you and with being a mom. And I thought, what would a mom like more than anything else? Then the answer came to me — *not* to be a mom for awhile. You know, to have a break. And *then* I thought, maybe we could give this present to a lot of the moms whose kids we sit for."

"Huh?" said Claudia.

"I guess I'm a little ahead of myself," I replied. (I'm usually a little ahead of myself.)

My friends shifted position and I looked at them as I tried to figure out how to explain my great idea. Mallory, with her new short haircut, was sitting on the floor, leaning against Claud's bed. She was wearing jeans with zippers up the bottoms of the legs, and a sweat shirt that said STONEYBROOK MIDDLE SCHOOL across the front. In her newly pierced ears were tiny gold hoops.

Jessi was wearing matching hoops (I think she and Mal had gone shopping together), a purple dance leotard, and jeans. Over the leotard she was wearing a purple-and-white striped shirt, unbuttoned.

On the bed, in a row, sat Mary Anne, Dawn, and Claudia, watching me intently. Mary Anne's hair was pulled back in a ponytail and held in place with a black-and-white checkered bow that matched the short skirt she was wearing. Around her neck was a chain and dangling from it were gold letters that spelled out MARY ANNE.

Dawn was wearing a necklace, too, only hers said I'M AWESOME. Honest. Where had she gotten it? California, probably. And in her *double* pierced ears were hoops of different sizes. See what I mean about Dawn being an individual? Also she was wearing a fairly tame dress, but on her feet were plaid high-top sneakers.

Then there was Claudia. She was wearing a pretty tame dress, too — with a red necktie! Then, she had on these new, very cool roll socks. When she pushed them down just right, they fell into three rolls. The top roll was red, the middle one was peacock blue, and the bottom one was purple. She looked as if she were wearing ice-cream cones on her feet. In her hair was a braided band in red, blue, and purple, like her socks. And dangling from her ears were — get this — spiders in webs. Ew. (But they were pretty cool.)

And me? I was wearing what I always wear — jeans, a turtleneck, a sweater, and sneakers. Okay, so I'm not a creative dresser. I don't have pierced ears, either. I'm sorry. That sort of thing just doesn't interest me much.

"My idea," I began, "is to give mothers a break in their routine. I thought that as a present to the mothers whose kids we sit for — you know, Mrs. Newton, Mrs. Perkins, Mrs. Barrett, some of our own mothers — we could take their kids off their hands for a day. We could do something really fun with the kids so they'd have a good time, and while they were gone, the mothers could enjoy some peace and quiet."

All around me, eyes were lighting up.

"Yeah!" said Claudia slowly.

"That's a great idea," agreed Jessi.

"Awesome," added Dawn.

Mal and Mary Anne were nodding their heads vigorously.

"Good idea?" I asked unnecessarily.

"The best," said Dawn.

I breathed a sigh of relief. Sometimes I get so carried away with my ideas that I can't tell whether they're good or stupid.

The phone rang then, and we stopped and arranged a sitting job for Jessi.

"I was thinking," I went on as Mary Anne put down the appointment book, "that we could take the kids on some kind of field trip. I mean, an outing. I don't know what kind exactly, but we'll come up with something. And maybe we could do this on the day before Mother's Day. That way, the present will be close to the actual holiday, but we'll still be able to spend Sunday with our own moth —"

I stopped abruptly. How could I be so thoughtless? I glanced at Mary Anne, who was looking down at her hands.

"With — with, um, our families," I finished up. I prayed for the phone to ring then, to save my neck and Mary Anne's feelings, but it didn't.

Instead, Jessi said, "If we're asking our little brothers and sisters on the outing, I *know* Becca would like to come. Especially if we invite Charlotte, too." (Charlotte Johanssen, one of our sitting charges, and Becca Ramsey are best friends.) "Becca might be shy, but she always likes a good field trip."

I smiled gratefully at Jessi. She meant what she'd just said, but I knew she'd only said it to take everyone's attention away from mothers and Mother's Day. Also, she got our discussion going again.

"My brothers and sisters would like a trip, too," spoke up Mal. "Well, most of them would. The triplets and Vanessa might think they're too old for this. But, well, what about money? If this really is a present to mo — to our clients, then I guess we're going to pay for everything, right?"

"We should talk about that," I replied. "I really haven't worked out all the details."

Ordinarily, I might have come up with some solution and said, "Okay, this is what we're going to do." But I know that I can be bossy. Sometimes it gets me in trouble. Not long ago, it nearly caused our whole club to break up. Well, maybe I'm exaggerating. But it did cause a huge fight.

So all I said was, "I don't think the day has to be very expensive. Maybe we could use money that's in the treasury. We have enough right now, don't we, Dawn?"

Dawn nodded.

"Okay, then. *But* — everyone has to agree to this. This isn't usually how we spend the treasury money."

We were in the middle of taking a vote when the phone rang. And rang and rang. We stopped to schedule a few jobs. Then we returned to the vote. It was unanimous. We agreed to use our treasury money.

"Now," I went on, "what should the outing be? I mean, where should we go? It should be someplace that's fun, but easy to get to and cheap."

We all thought. No one came up with a single idea. There isn't a lot to do here in Stoneybrook. Not a lot that's within walking distance anyway.

Claudia cleared her throat and we looked at her expectantly. "I don't have an idea," she said. "I was just thinking that the way we could ask kids to come on the outing would be to send invitations to their mothers. I think the outing would seem more like a gift then. An invitation could say, 'Happy Mother's Day, Mrs. Rodowsky. As a special present, the Baby-sitters Club would like to give you a day to yourself. Therefore, Jackie, Archie, and Shea are invited to go' . . . wherever we decide to go. Something like that."

"Ooh, that's great, Claud," said Jessi.

"Yeah," agreed Dawn. "Would you design the invitations, Claud? We'll help you make them, but you do the best artwork."

"Thanks," replied Claudia. "Sure. I'll design something."

"Maybe the fathers could be involved," I said slowly. "I'm not sure how to get them to do this, but they should be the ones to drop the kids off and pick them up. Stuff like that. And of course we can't take babies on the outing. So, for instance, if we take Jamie Newton for the day, Lucy will still be at home. Maybe Mr. Newton will agree to watch her while Jamie's with us."

My friends nodded. We talked and talked. We talked until it was after six o'clock. We worked out all the details, but not what our outing would be. Where could we take the kids?

"You know," said Jessi, as we were getting ready to leave Claud's room, "I think our Mother's Day surprise solves a problem for me."

"What?" asked the rest of us.

"I think it can be my present to Mama. It'll get Becca *and* me out of her hair for a whole day. And if Daddy will watch Squirt, then Mama will really have a vacation."

"Same here," said Mal. "The younger kids can come on the trip, and I'm sure I can convince the triplets and Vanessa to stay out of Mom's hair. Or maybe Dad can do something with them."

"And same with me," I added. "Andrew, Karen, and David Michael will come with us. Charlie and Sam are hardly ever around on Saturdays anyway. I *think* this will be my gift. I'll just have to see."

"I wish the outing helped me," said Dawn with a sigh, "but it doesn't."

"Me neither," added Claudia. "All I've decided is to *make* Mom's gift, whatever it will be."

"Maybe I'll make mine, too," said Dawn. "Would you help me, Claud?"

"Sure."

We were filing out of Claudia's room, tired but excited.

Mary Anne was being awfully quiet, but just as I was starting to worry about her, she gave me a little smile to let me know that she would handle Mother's Day somehow — just as she had handled it every year before.

CHAPTER 5

Friday

I babysat for Jamie newton today
guess waht. Thanks to jamie I think I
discovered the place wher we can take
the kids for there outing. Jamie was in
the bake yard and he was printinding
to be in circas or something. He was
printinding to walk on a thight rope
and be a clowne and stuff. Then I took
him inside for a glas of water and
guess waht I saw. It looked like the
anser to our probelms.

Claudia's job at the Newtons' on Friday afternoon turned out to be profitable. Not only
did she have fun and get paid, but she found

something pretty interesting. It was a flyer posted on their refrigerator.

Well, once again I'm ahead of myself. I bet you don't have any idea what I'm talking about. (I don't blame you.) Okay. Let me go back to when Claud arrived at the Newtons'.

She showed up on time, of course. (A good sitter is *always* on time.) But she didn't bring her Kid-Kit. It was a sunny afternoon and she knew that all Jamie would want to do was play outside.

Mrs. Newton greeted Claudia at the door.

"Hi, honey," she said. "Come on in."

"Thanks." Claudia stepped into the Newtons' hallway.

"How are you? How are the art classes?" asked Mrs. Newton. She and Claud are pretty close. Mrs. Newton is interested in whatever Claudia does.

"I'm fine. My classes are great. And look what I made." Claudia pulled her hair back to show Mrs. Newton the earrings she was wearing. They were painted sunbursts.

"You *made* those?"

"Yup," said Claudia proudly.

Mrs. Newton shook her head in amazement.

"Where are the kids?" asked Claud.

"Jamie's out in the yard, and Lucy's upstairs taking a nap. I just put her down, so she should sleep for awhile. You can go out with Jamie, but stick your head inside every now and then to listen for the baby."

Claudia nodded. "Okay. Anything else?"

"I don't think so. You know where the emergency numbers are. And I'll be at a meeting at Jamie's school. The number is on the refrigerator."

A few minutes later, Mrs. Newton called goodbye to Jamie and left. Claudia joined Jamie in the backyard. She found him tiptoeing around with his arms outstretched. He was singing "Home on the Range," but he was getting a lot of the words wrong.

"Oh, give me a comb," he sang loudly, *"where the buffaloes foam, and the deer and the antinope pay. Where seldom is heard a long-distance bird, and the sky is not crowded all day."*

Claudia smiled, but she managed not to laugh. "Hiya, Jamie," she said.

"Hi-hi!" Jamie replied happily. He didn't seem to mind having been interrupted at all.

"What are you doing?" Claud wanted to know. (Jamie was still tiptoeing around.)

"I'm a tightrope walker. Now watch this. I'm going to be someone else."

Jamie walked a few steps. He tripped and fell. Then he picked himself up and fell again. When he stood up, he shook himself all over like a puppy dog.

Claudia wasn't sure what was going on, so she was relieved when Jamie began turning somersaults and making silly faces. "You're a clown!" she exclaimed.

"Right!" said Jamie. "And now I'm going to be another person."

He raised his arms in the air and ran back and forth across the yard. *"Oh, he fries food the air,"* he sang, *"with the greatest of vease!"*

"A trapeze artist," said Claud.

"Yup."

The Newtons must have gone to a circus, she thought. And she thought that until she took Jamie inside for a glass of water. His throat was dry from all his singing and running around. Claud went to the refrigerator to get out the bottle of cold water she knew was inside — and her eyes fell on a colorful flyer posted next to the phone number of Jamie's school.

COME TO SUDSY'S CARNIVAL! it read. GAMES! RIDES! SIDESHOW ATTRACTIONS! REFRESHMENTS!

Carefully, Claudia read every word on the

flyer. The carnival would be in Stoneybrook on Mother's Day weekend. It would be set up in a large parking lot that was near a playground not far from Claud's house. It would have midway games, some rides, plenty of food (cotton candy, peanuts, ice cream, popcorn, lemonade), and even a sideshow. Claudia raised her eyebrows. Were there *really* people who could swallow fire or swords? She wasn't sure. But she didn't care. All she was interested in was finding out more about the carnival.

Jamie saw Claud looking at the flyer. "The carnival," he said sadly.

"What's wrong?" asked Claud.

"I really really really really really want to go, but I can't. Mommy and Daddy can't take me."

"Too bad, Jamie," said Claudia.

"I know. I want to see that man. That one right there."

Jamie reached up to touch a picture of a clown carrying a bunch of helium balloons.

"The balloon-seller?" Claudia asked.

Jamie nodded. "I would buy a yellow balloon. Maybe after that I would buy a green balloon for Lucy."

"That would be very generous of you."

"And then I would play some games. I would win some prizes, like a whistle and a teddy bear. The bear would be for Lucy, too."

Claudia smiled.

"But," Jamie continued with a sigh, "I guess I can't go. No clowns. No balloons. No prizes."

Claudia gave Jamie a hug, and then poured him his glass of water.

"Thank you," he said politely.

"You're welcome. And Jamie, you never know."

"What?"

"You never know about things. You can't be too sure. I remember once when I was seven, a big circus came to Stamford, and Mom and Dad said our whole family could go. Only — a week before we were going to the circus, I got the chicken pox."

"Yuck."

"I know. And when circus day came, I was much better but I still had spots, so I wasn't allowed to go. Mimi took care of me while Mom and Dad and Janine went to the circus. Guess what, though. People liked the circus so much that it stayed an extra week, and Mimi and I went to it the next Saturday."

"*Really?* Wow."

Claudia suddenly realized that she shouldn't get Jamie's hopes up *too* much. After all, the carnival was still sort of a long shot. So she said again, "You just never know, Jamie. I'm not saying you will go to the carnival. But it's several weeks away. A lot could happen, right? . . . Right?"

"Oh, give me a comb. . . ."

Jamie wasn't listening. He and Claudia went back outside. Jamie played carnival again. Every now and then, Claudia tiptoed into the house and stood at the bottom of the stairs, listening for Lucy. The third time she did that, she heard baby sounds. Lucy almost always wakes up happy. She doesn't cry. She just sits in her crib and talks to herself in words only she can understand.

Claudia poked her head out the back door. "Jamie!" she called. "Come on inside. I have to get Lucy up."

Jamie came in and found *Sesame Street* on the television, while Claudia dashed upstairs. She opened the door to Lucy's room slowly.

"Hiya, Lucy-Goose," she said.

Lucy's face began to crumple.

"I know. I'm not your mommy or daddy. I'm sorry. But it's me, Luce. It's Claudee." (That's what Jamie sometimes calls Claudia.)

Claudia puttered around Lucy's room, not going too near her. She sang "The Eensy Weensy Spider" and "The Wheels on the Bus."

Lucy began to smile. Claudia tickled her and changed her diaper, and she seemed to be okay. So Claud carried her downstairs. She could smell Lucy's baby smell — powder and Pampers and soap and milk.

"Jamie, look who's here!" said Claudia.

Jamie turned away from the TV. When he and Lucy saw each other, their faces broke into grins.

What a change from when Lucy first came home from the hospital, thought Claudia. Jamie wanted to send his sister back.

Claudia, Jamie, and Lucy played on the floor of the family room until Mrs. Newton came home at five-fifteen. Then Claudia raced to her own house for our Friday meeting. She couldn't wait to get there. For once, she would be the one with a big idea, and if everyone liked it, she'd make a lot of people very happy — especially Jamie Newton, who just might get to go to the carnival and see the balloon-seller after all.

CHAPTER 6

For the second time in a row I arrived at our meeting early. There was a good reason for this. It was because I had begged Charlie to leave early. "Please, please, please take me over now," I'd said. My next step would have been to kneel down and plead, but Charlie agreed to go.

I don't know why I was so eager for the meeting. It wasn't as if I had any news. I just wanted to get on with the plans for our Mother's Day surprise.

Anyway, thanks to Charlie, I reached the Kishis' just before Claudia came running home from the Newtons'. I could hear her calling to me as she dashed along the sidewalk.

"Hi, Claud!" I replied. I stood on her steps and looked across the street at the house that used to be mine. I'd grown up there. I'd learned to walk and ride a bike and turn cartwheels there. I'd gone off to school and watched my father walk out on us and seen Watson come into our lives. I'd been away from that house for less than a year, but it seemed like a decade.

Time is funny.

Claudia raced up her walk and let me into her house. "You're early again," she said. "Do you have news?"

I shook my head.

"Well, I do! But I guess it'll have to wait until the meeting starts, right?"

"Not necessarily," I replied, since I was dying of curiosity, "but I guess you might as well. Then you can tell us all at once."

Claudia and I were both a little disappointed, but at least we didn't have long to wait before the meeting started. Mary Anne, Jessi, Dawn, and Mallory arrived on time, and I brought us to order immediately.

"The first piece of business," I announced, "is that Claudia has some sort of big news. Claudia?" I said, turning to her.

"My big news," Claudia began, shifting position on the bed, "is that I think I've found a place where we can take the kids on their outing."

Five pairs of eyes widened. The room was absolutely silent.

Then I cried out, "Where, where, *where*?" I couldn't help it.

"To a carnival," Claud began. "See, I was sitting at the Newtons' this afternoon, and on their refrigerator was a flyer advertising something called Sudsy's Carnival. It's going to be in Stoneybrook the weekend of Mother's Day. There'll be all sorts of things kids will like — games, rides, even a sideshow. But the best thing is, guess where the carnival will be set up?"

"Where?" asked all the rest of us club members.

"In the parking lot near Carle Playground."

"Oh, wow!" I exclaimed. "We can walk there easily!"

"Right," said Claud. "And it seems like a nice, small carnival. I mean, it wouldn't be overwhelming for the littlest kids, and we'd have an easy time keeping track of everyone."

"I wonder how expensive a carnival would be," said our treasurer. "Any idea what it would cost per kid?"

I looked at Claudia.

"It's hard to say," she replied slowly. "The flyer didn't mention a fee to get in — you know, the way you pay one big price to get into Funland,

and then you can go on the rides as often as you want. I guess one fee wouldn't make sense at a carnival anyway, since so much of it is games that you have to pay for separately." Claud paused. She drew in her breath. "I'm guessing the carnival wouldn't be too expensive per kid. There's an awful lot just to look at, and if we limit the kids to, say, three things each, that wouldn't be too bad."

We asked Claudia a few more questions, but everyone in the room was smiling. We knew we had the solution to our problem, and what a solution it was!

"Jamie is going to *faint*!" exclaimed Claudia. "He's dying to go to Sudsy's."

"I don't think David Michael has ever been to a carnival," I added.

"Becca has," said Jessi, "and when she gets to this one, she'll think she's died and gone to heaven."

"I wonder if the kids will be able to spend all day at a carnival," I said suddenly. "That just occurred to me."

"Hmm," said Mary Anne. "Maybe not. Especially if they can only do a few things each."

"I don't think *I* could spend all day at a carnival," spoke up Dawn. "I was just at one when

I visited Dad and Jeff in California. It was fun, but . . ."

"All day at anything is too long for little kids," I pointed out. "They need to rest. They get bored."

"Maybe," began Mallory, but she was interrupted by the phone.

We arranged several sitting jobs. Then Mallory started again.

"Maybe we should just go to the carnival in the morning when everyone is fresh and awake," she said. "Then we could eat lunch somewhere else, like at the playground, since the kids are bringing their lunches anyway, and we'll be right next to the playground. There are tables and benches everywhere at Carle. Our family has taken a lot of picnic lunches there."

"That's a good idea," I said. "Really good. Then the kids could play in the park for awhile, and then we really should give them a chance to rest before they go home."

"Well," said Claudia, "they *could* come to my house. Remember last summer when we ran the play group in Stacey's backyard? We could do something like that here. It would probably be for just an hour or two. We could read stories and maybe do an art project. The kids could make Mother's Day cards or little gifts or something. It would be a nice way for them to unwind after all the excitement."

"Great!" I exclaimed. "I think we've got our Mother's Day surprise." Then I remembered about being bossy and added, "Everyone who thinks this is a good plan, raise her hand."

Five hands shot up, including mine.

"Dawn? What's wrong? You didn't raise your hand."

Dawn grinned. "I don't think it's a good plan," she said. "I think it's an awesome one."

Everyone laughed, and Claudia threw a pillow at Dawn.

"Okay," I said, when we had quieted down, "I know we don't have much time left today, but I think we should make a list of kids to invite so we can get the invitations out soon. There really isn't *that* much time until Mother's Day."

"I'll take notes," said our secretary. Mary Anne turned to a blank page in the back of the record book. "All right. I'm ready."

"Let's start with our little brothers and sisters," I began. "Karen, Andrew, and David Michael will be invited. And Becca Ramsey. And . . . Mal, who in your family?"

"I guess everyone except the triplets. Claire, Margo, Nicky, and Vanessa. I'm really not sure

Vanessa will come, though. She's funny about big group things sometimes. She'd rather stay in her room and write poetry."

Mary Anne nodded. "Well, if she comes, that's eight so far."

"Jamie Newton," said Claudia.

"The Barretts," said Dawn. "Buddy and Suzi, anyway. Marnie's too little."

"Myriah and Gabbie Perkins," added Mary Anne, writing furiously. "And, of course, Laura is much too little."

"The Rodowsky boys," spoke up Jessi. "Oh, and the Braddock kids. How could we forget them?"

"I hate to say this," said Mary Anne, "but Jenny Prezzioso. We just *have* to ask her if we ask the Barretts and Mal's brothers and sisters."

"Oh, ew!" I cried. "Ew, *EW*! Jenny is so spoiled." But I knew Mary Anne was right. So Jenny's name was added to the list.

We kept on thinking of kids to invite — Charlotte Johanssen, some kids in my new neighborhood. When we couldn't come up with another name, I said to Mary Anne, "What's the grand total?"

Mary Anne counted up. "Oh, my gosh! Twenty-nine!"

"Twenty-nine!" exclaimed Claudia. "We're good baby-sitters, but the six of us cannot take twenty-nine kids to a carnival."

There was a moment of silence. Then Jessi said, "Well, they won't *all* be able to come. Mal said Vanessa probably won't want to, and some people are bound to be away that day, or to have plans."

"True . . ." I replied slowly. "Even so. Let's say twenty kids want to go on the outing. There are six of us. Some of us would have to be in charge of four kids all day. That's pretty many. And what if we end up with more kids than we think?"

"Well, how about calling our associate members?" suggested Mary Anne, grinning. (You could tell she was just dying to call Logan.)

"Maybe we better." I handed the phone to Mary Anne. She called Logan. His family was going to be out of town that weekend.

Mary Anne handed the phone back to me. I called Shannon Kilbourne. *Her* family would be having weekend guests. Shannon was supposed to stick around and be polite.

"Uh-oh," I said when I'd hung up the phone.

"Wait a second!" cried Claudia. "Oh, my lord! I've got a great idea. Let's call Stacey and invite her to Stoneybrook for the weekend!"

As if you couldn't tell from Claudia's excite-ment, she and Stacey McGill used to be best friends. (Well, they still are but it's difficult with Claud living in Stoneybrook and Stacey living in New York City.) Anyway, I knew we all wanted to see Stacey, and she's a terrific baby-sitter.

Claudia made the call. "Stace? It's me," she said. A whole lot of screaming and laughing fol-lowed. Then Claudia explained about the Mother's Day surprise. "So could you come?" she asked. "We aren't getting paid or anything. It would just be fun. And you could stay for awhile on Sunday before we put you on the train back to the city."

Stacey had to check with her parents, but guess what — she got permission!

"You can come?" shrieked Claudia. She turned to us club members. "She's free! She can come! . . . Stace? We'll make the arrangements later. Oh, I'm *so glad*! This will be your first trip back to Stoneybrook."

Well, it had been your basic red-letter club meeting. By the time Claud got off the phone, it was just after six, so we had to leave, but all of us felt as if we were floating instead of walking. We agreed to return to Claudia's the next day, Saturday, to make the invitations.

CHAPTER 7

The arrangements for the Mother's Day surprise were falling into place. Claudia's parents had spoken to Stacey's parents, and the adults had decided that Stacey would take the train to Stoneybrook on Friday after school. With any luck, she'd reach the Kishis' in time for our club meeting that day! Then she would stay with Claud until Sunday afternoon — and help us out on Saturday, of course.

Also our invitations had been designed, made, and mailed out. They were pretty cute, if I do say so myself. Claud had drawn two pictures on them. In the upper lefthand corner was a totally dragged-out looking mom. She was holding a briefcase in one hand and a vacuum cleaner in the other, and a baby was strapped to her chest. Her hair looked frazzled and there were bags under her eyes. In the lower righthand corner was a rested mom. She was sitting in a lawn chair with a book in one hand and a glass of iced tea (or something) in the other. She was smiling, and the bags were gone.

In the middle of the page, we had written: "SURPRISE! Happy Mother's Day! The members of the Baby-sitters Club would like to give our special moms a special gift."

(I thought that part was corny, but no one agreed with me.)

Then the invitations went on to say who was invited, what we would do, where we would meet, and that sort of thing.

I was at home on the Saturday my own mom received her Mother's Day surprise. It was one of those gorgeous spring days when you look at the sky and think, Could it possibly get any bluer? It was also unusually warm, so David Michael, Andrew, Karen, and I were out in our yard with no jackets or sweaters.

"It's summer! It's just like summer!" exclaimed Karen.

We still had a good two months before vacation, but I didn't say anything.

The kids were doing the outdoor things they missed during the winter, like skipping rope, tossing a ball around, and turning somersaults. Mom and Watson were inside. They were on the phone. They'd been making an awful lot of phone calls lately. And Sam and Charlie, as usual, were off with their friends.

Sometimes I feel . . . I don't know . . . left out of my own family. I love everybody, but I'm too young to hang around with Sam and Charlie, and too old for Andrew, David Michael, and Karen. They're fun, but they *are* just kids.

Anyway, David Michael's game of catch with Andrew was beginning to get out of hand.

"David Michael," I said, "you don't have to throw it so hard. Andrew's not that far away from you."

"But, he keeps missing the balls."

"Maybe he's afraid of them. They're coming at him like freight trains."

"I'm not afraid!" protested Andrew.

I sighed. Since I wasn't baby-sitting, I didn't feel like getting involved in this argument. "I think I'll take Shannon on a walk," I said.

Shannon was playing in the yard, but I knew she'd want to take a walk. Any change of scenery was fine with her. I clipped her leash to her collar and we set off. I chose one particular direction. It was the direction in which Bart Taylor's house lies.

Bart Taylor is nice. Oh, okay, he's gorgeous and wonderful and smart and athletic. We sort of like each other, even though we don't go to the same school. Bart coaches a softball team called Bart's Bashers, and I coach one called Kristy's Krushers. So Bart is my rival, too. We try not to think of that. But we hardly ever see each other anyway.

Which is why I walked Shannon by his house that day. I tried to glance at it casually every few steps, but I couldn't see a thing that way. So finally I just stared. The front door was closed, the shades were drawn, the garage door was pulled down.

No one was home.

I walked Shannon sadly back to my house, feeling lonely and a little depressed. But the warm weather and the thought of the weekend stretching before me cheered me up again.

"Hey, you guys!" I called when I reached our yard. "How about some batting practice? The Krushers have another game coming up!"

Andrew, David Michael, and Karen are on my softball team. That ought to give you some idea of what the team is like. It's a bunch of kids who are either too young for Little League or even T-ball, or who are too embarrassed to belong to one of those teams — but who really want to learn to play better. The first time the Krushers played Bart's Bashers we almost beat them. That's how much spirit we have.

"Batting practice?" echoed Karen. "Okay. Let's go."

We found several bats and two softballs.

"I'll be the pitcher," I said. "We're going to work on your technique. David Michael, show me your batting stance, okay?"

My brother demonstrated.

"Good!" I cried. "That's really terrific." No doubt about it, my brother had improved since I'd started coaching him. I don't mean to sound conceited, but it was true.

I tossed the ball — underhand, easy.

David Michael missed it by a mile.

I take it back. Maybe he was still a klutz.

"Karen?" I called. "Your turn."

Karen was testing the weights of the bats when Mom dashed into the backyard, waving a paper in her hand.

Oh, *darn*, I thought. Which one of us messed up? What was she waving? A math test with an F on the top? A report with the words "See me" in red ink? (I swear, those are the worst words teachers ever invented.)

"Kristy!" Mom called.

Yikes! It was *me*! I had messed up!

"Honey, thank you," said my mother breathlessly as she reached me.

Thank you? Well, I couldn't have done anything too bad. I dared to look at the paper. It was the Mother's Day surprise. *Whew.*

"You're welcome," I replied, smiling.

Mom put her arms around me.

"It's your Mother's Day surprise," I said unnecessarily.

Immediately, Mom began to cry. It wasn't that sobbing, unhappy crying that mothers do when they're watching something like *Love Story* or *Brian's Song* on TV. It was that teary kind of crying where the voice just goes all wavery. "Wha-at a lo-ovely invita-ation," she managed to squeak out. She wiped at her eyes. Then she found a tissue stuffed up her sleeve, so she blew her nose.

(Well, I knew the invitations were nice, but I hadn't expected this. I would have to call Jessi and Mallory to find out if their mothers had freaked out, too.)

"Um, Mom," I began, gathering my nerve to ask the question that so far only Sam had dared to ask, "are you pregnant?"

My mother shook her head. She blew her nose again. "No."

"Are you positive?"

"Positive. . . . But if you were to have a new brother or sister, how —"

"Well, you know how I feel about kids, Mom," I said. "It would be fine."

But suddenly it didn't seem quite as fine as it had seemed in the past. I love babies. I really do. But what would it be like if Mom and Watson had a baby of their own? That would be different from Mrs. Newton or Mrs. Perkins having a baby. It might draw Mom and Watson closer together — and shut us kids out, just when us kids need to be drawn closer to everyone in the family. Why hadn't I thought about that before? But all I said was, "Fine, fine."

Mom smiled. The two of us sat down in the grass. "So tell me more about this invitation," said my mother. "Who planned the surprise?"

"Everyone in the Baby-sitters Club," I answered, "only, the basic idea was sort of mine. Well, it was all mine."

"I'm sure it was. You always did have big ideas."

"Remember when we lived in the old house, and I worked out the flashlight code so Mary Anne and I could talk to each other from our bedroom windows at night?"

"Of course. And your big idea to marry me to the mailman?"

"David Michael wanted a father," I reminded her. "I was only ten then."

Mom and I laughed. We watched Andrew, Karen, and David Michael practice their pitching and catching.

"Well, anyway," I said, "we sent out invitations to twenty-nine kids."

"Twenty-nine!" squawked Mom.

"Don't worry. They won't all be able to come. Besides, Stacey is going to be in town that weekend. She's going to help us. So there'll be seven sitters. If we wind up with, let's say, twenty kids, that's only about three kids per sitter. We can handle that."

"And you're taking the children to a carnival?"

"Yup. It's called Sudsy's. It's just a little one. It'll be set up in that big parking lot near Carle Playground. We'll spend the morning at Sudsy's, go to the playground for lunch and some exercise, then walk back to Claudia's house for stories and stuff, so the kids can rest. We figure we'll have the kids from about nine until four. That'll be a nice rest for you, won't it, Mom?"

"A wonderful one."

The phone rang then. We could hear it through the open kitchen window. A moment later,

Watson called, "Elizabeth? This is an important one."

My mother leaped to her feet like an Olympic athlete and dashed inside.

I went back to my sister and brothers.

"How are you guys doing?" I asked. I asked it before I saw the scowls on the kids' faces.

"He is a klutz," said David Michael with clenched teeth, pointing to Andrew.

"Am not."

"Are too, you little wimp. And you're Watson's favorite."

"No, he isn't," cried Karen indignantly. "Daddy loves us both the same."

"What about *me*?" David Michael threw his bat angrily to the ground.

Karen and Andrew did the same thing. Softballs, too.

"Well, I guess it figures," my brother went on. "Of course he loves you guys more than me. He's your real father. He's just my step."

"Your mom loves you more than us," spoke up Andrew, to my surprise. "She's *our* step."

"*Hey, hey, HEY!* What is this talk?" I cried. "Everybody loves everybody around here."

"No," said David Michael. "Sometimes

Thomases love Thomases more, and Brewers love Brewers more."

Karen sighed. "I'm tired of this. Let's play ball again."

The kids picked up their bats. They forgot their argument for awhile.

But I didn't.

CHAPTER 8

"Well, it's finally happened!" I announced.

"What?" asked Claudia, Jessi, Dawn, Mary Anne, and Mallory.

We were holding a meeting of the Baby-sitters Club, and the last of the RSVPs for the Mother's Day surprise had just been phoned in. I gave the news to my friends.

"We can get a total count now," I said. "That was Mrs. Barrett. Buddy and Suzi can come on the outing. They were the last kids we needed to hear about. Mary Anne?"

Mary Anne had opened the record book to a page on which she was listing the kids who'd be coming to Sudsy's with us. "Ready for the total?" she asked.

The rest of us nodded nervously.

"Okay, just a sec." Mary Anne's pen moved down the page. Then, "It's twenty-one," she announced.

"Twenty-one! That's perfect!" I cried. "Seven sitters including Stacey, so three kids each. We can manage that."

"Sure," said Dawn.

"We can help each other out," added Claudia.

"Read us the list, Mary Anne," I said. "Let's see exactly what we're dealing with here."

"Okay." Mary Anne began reading, running her finger along the list. "Claire, Margo, Nicky, and Vanessa Pike." (Vanessa had surprised everyone by immediately agreeing to come.) "Becca Ramsey; David Michael Thomas; Karen and Andrew Brewer; Jamie Newton; Jackie, Shea, and Archie Rodowsky; Jenny Prezzioso." (I tried not to choke.) "Myriah and Gabbie Perkins; Matt and Haley Braddock; Charlotte Johanssen; Nina Marshall; and Buddy and Suzi Barrett."

"And who couldn't come?" I asked.

"Let's see," said Mary Anne, turning to another page in the record book, "the Arnold twins, Betsy Sobak, the Papadakises, and the Delaneys."

I nodded. "Okay. I was just curious."

Ring, ring.

Dawn reached for the phone. "Hello, Baby-sitters Club," she said. "Yes, hi, Mrs. Arnold. . . . Oh, we're sorry, too. The twins would probably love

Sudsy's. . . . Yeah. . . . Yeah. . . . Okay, on Tuesday? I'll check. I'll call you right back."

We arranged for Mal to sit for Marilyn and Carolyn Arnold (can you believe their names?) on Tuesday afternoon. Then we went back to our work.

"I guess we should make up groups of kids for the outing," said Claudia. "That worked well before."

Once, our club had sat for fourteen kids for a whole week. We kept the kids in groups according to their ages. It was really helpful. And we had done the same thing when Mary Anne, Dawn, Claudia, and I had visited Stacey in New York and taken a big group of kids to a museum and to Central Park.

"The only thing," spoke up Mary Anne, "is that I'm not sure we should group the kids by age. I think we should group them, but, well, Matt and Haley will have to be in the same group, even though Matt is seven and Haley's almost ten now. Haley understands Matt's signing better than anybody." (Matt is Deaf and communicates using sign language.)

"And," I added, "I think Karen and Andrew should be in the same group, and David Michael should be in a different one. Andrew is really dependent on Karen, and lately the two of them have been having some problems with David Michael."

"And Charlotte and Becca *have* to be together," added Jessi. "Becca won't come if she can't be with Charlotte."

"Hmm," I said. "Anything else?"

"Keep Jenny away from the Braddocks," said Dawn.

"And Nicky away from Claire," added Mallory.

"Boy, is this complicated," commented Claudia.

"I know," I agreed. "But we can do it. Let's try to draw up some lists. Let's just see how far we get. Everyone, make up seven lists and then we'll compare them."

Mary Anne passed around paper and we set to work. We were interrupted four times by the telephone, but at last everyone said they had done the best they could.

I collected the papers. I looked over the groups my friends had come up with. I said things like, "No, that one won't work. Matt and Haley aren't together." Or, "Oh, that's good, that's good, that's — Nope. We've got Claire and Nicky together."

"I've got an idea," said Dawn after awhile.

"Why don't you cut out all the groups, all forty-two of them, sort through them, and try to find the seven best?"

"Okay," I agreed. Claudia handed me a pair of scissors. "But I think I'll need some help."

Every single club member got down on her hands and knees. We spread the lists on the floor, examined them, and shuffled them around.

"This is a good one," said Jessi.

"This is a good one," said Claud.

Finally we had chosen seven good lists. We counted the kids. Twenty-one. We checked the kids against Mary Anne's list. Nina Marshall showed up twice; Shea Rodowsky was missing.

"Darn it!" I cried.

We started over. Finally, finally, finally we had seven lists that worked:

Kristy	*Claudia*
Karen Brewer	Myriah Perkins
Andrew Brewer	Gabbie Perkins
Shea Rodowsky	Jamie Newton

Mary Anne	*Dawn*
Jenny Prezzioso	Suzi Barrett
Claire Pike	Nina Marshall
Margo Pike	Archie Rodowsky

Jessi
Matt Braddock
Haley Braddock
Nicky Pike

Mallory
Buddy Barrett
D. M. Thomas
Jackie Rodowsky

Stacey
Charlotte Johanssen
Becca Ramsey
Vanessa Pike

"Well," I said, "we've got all the necessary combinations — Matt and his sister are together, so are Charlotte and Becca, Jenny is separated from the Braddocks, and that sort of thing. There are some good combinations here, too. Like, Jamie and the Perkins girls are together, and they're friends. And I think Jenny will work out okay with Claire and Margo, don't you, Mal?"

"Yeah, that should be all right."

"But," I went on, "there are some odd combinations here, too. Not bad, just odd. For instance, Shea Rodowsky is with Karen and Andrew. Shea is nine. He's a lot older than they are. But where else could we put him?"

The six of us leaned over to examine the lists.

"I don't really see any place," said Dawn after a moment. "Claudia's group, Mary Anne's, and mine are too young. Stacey's is all girls. Jessi's is perfect the way it is. Mallory's would be good because the kids are all boys, but they're younger than Shea, too. Besides, I wouldn't mind separating Shea and Jackie."

"Here's another odd list," said Claudia. "I'm not sure what Archie Rodowsky will think of Suzi and Nina. At least the three of them are about the same age."

"I think we've made good choices about the baby-sitter in charge of each group," Mary Anne pointed out. "Kristy, Andrew would want to be with you."

I nodded. "I know."

"And Claud, you're a good choice for Jamie and the Perkins girls. I think I'm the only one who will handle Jenny. Dawn knows Suzi Barrett really well. Jessi *has* to stick with Matt and Haley since she's the only one of us who knows sign language really well. Mallory will be good with the boys, and Charlotte Johanssen will just *die* to have her old sitter back. Remember how much she loved Stacey?"

"Boy, do I!" I said. I looked at the lists a few moments longer. "Okay," I said at last. "We know the groups are going to get all mixed up anyway, but they *will* be helpful. And I think these are the best we're going to do. Do you guys agree?"

"Yes!" It was unanimous.

"Gosh, this is so exciting!" cried Mary Anne.

"Yeah!" agreed Jessi. "It's the first big Baby-sitters Club project I've been part of."

"Me, too," said Mal.

"And I'll finally get to meet Stacey," Jessi went on. "It's so funny to think that I live in her old house — that I *sleep* in her old *bedroom* — and I've never even met her."

"Well, it won't be long now," said Claudia.

"How many of these big — I mean, really big — projects has the club worked on?" Mal wondered.

"Three, I think. Right, Kristy?" answered Dawn. "There was the week before your mom and Watson got married when we took care of the fourteen kids, and there was the play group in Stacey's backyard, and then there was New Yor —"

Ring, ring.

Mary Anne answered the phone while Dawn kept talking. But after about a minute we realized we were listening to Mary Anne instead of Dawn.

"You won't *believe* this!" Mary Anne was saying. (I guessed the caller was not a client.) "We were just talking about New York. Dawn was going to tell about when we took the kids to the museum."

"Is that Stacey?" Claudia cried suddenly. She scrambled off the bed.

I could feel excitement mounting. Stacey! Our old club member! Soon the club would be together again. Actually, when I thought about it, I realized the club would be together again for the first time — because the seven of us had never worked together. Jessi and Mal had joined the club after Stacey had left.

Claudia and Stacey talked to each other.

Then I got on the phone with Stace. "Hi! How *are* you? I can't wait till you get here. We are going to have such a great day. You won't believe how some of the kids have changed. Andrew is so much taller! Oh, and you can meet Matt and Haley Braddock and Becca Ramsey. And Jessi, of course."

"Same old Kristy," said Stacey, and I could tell she was smiling. "I'm fine. Mom and Dad have been arguing, arguing, arguing, but it's just a phase, I think. At least they aren't arguing about *me*."

Stacey has diabetes and her parents sometimes don't agree about the way Stacey manages her disease, even when she's following doctor's orders.

"What are they arguing about?" I asked.

"Oh, who cares? I can't wait to get back to Stoneybrook. Mom wishes she could come with me. She loves Connecticut. What's up with you?"

"Get this. *My* mom wants to have a baby."

"No!"

"Yeah. She and Watson want a baby. Can you imagine? I think they're too old," I said, which I knew wasn't true at all.

I changed the subject quickly, and Stacey and I talked a little longer. I told her about the day we'd planned, and about the groups we'd lined up. By the time we got off the phone, I was just as excited as Claudia about seeing our blonde-haired, blue-eyed, super-sophisticated former treasurer.

CHAPTER 9

"Aughh!"

"I don't believe it!"

"Oh, my gosh. She's here!"

"IT'S STACEY, YOU GUYS!"

It was 5:25 on the day before the Mother's Day surprise. Mary Anne, Dawn, and I had just entered Claudia's room for a club meeting — and found Claudia and Stacey there. Stacey was sitting on Claud's bed, as if she'd never left Stoneybrook. Claud was the one who'd shouted, "IT'S STACEY, YOU GUYS!"

Stacey leaped up, and she and I and Mary Anne and Dawn began hugging and jumping up and down — a group hug. And then we all began talking at once.

"You're here in time for the meeting!" I exclaimed.

"When did you get here?" Mary Anne wanted to know.

"Just a little while ago," replied Stace. "I caught an early train."

"You cut your hair!" Dawn cried.

"Yeah, a little. Do you like it? I went to this really punk place and told the guy not to make it too punk."

"We love it!" said Mary Anne, speaking for all of us.

We were finding places and settling down. I sat in the director's chair, of course. Dawn and Mary Anne squeezed onto the bed with Claudia and Stacey. We left room on the floor for Mal and Jessi.

"This is just so incredible," said Stacey. "Here I am, sitting in on a meeting of the Baby-sitters Club. A *real* meeting, not like the ones we had when you guys came to visit in New York. I feel like I never left here."

"I wish you never had," said Claud wistfully.

Stacey leaned over suddenly and put her arms around Claudia. Claud is not a big crier, but that hug was all it took for the tears to start to fall.

"I miss you so much," she said to Stace. And I knew what she *wasn't* saying: that Stacey was Claud's first and only best friend. And that she hadn't made a new best friend since Stacey had left.

It was while this was going on that I glanced up and saw Jessi and Mallory hovering uncertainly in the doorway to club headquarters. Jessi looked confused, and Mallory looked bewildered.

"Come on in, you guys," I said loudly to our two junior officers. "This isn't going to be a cry-fest . . . is it, Claud?"

Claudia pulled herself together. She wiped her tears with a tissue and sat up as straight as she could.

And Stacey slid off the bed. "Mal!" she exclaimed. "I am *so* glad to see you! Congratulations on becoming a club member."

"Thanks, Stacey. Baby-sitting sure is more fun this way. It's nice to be official."

Stacey turned to Jessi. "I guess you're Jessi Ramsey," she said.

This comment was a little unnecessary. For one thing, Stacey knows that Jessi is Black. I'm sorry to be so blunt, but that's the truth, and anyway I'm always blunt. Besides, who else would Jessi be? We don't bring guests to meetings.

"Yes," said Jessi. "Hi. I moved into your bedroom."

We laughed at that.

"Jessi is a terrific sitter," I said, as Stacey returned to the bed, and Jessi and Mal dropped to the floor. "She even learned sign language so she could communicate with a Deaf boy."

"Matt Braddock," added Jessi, looking a little embarrassed by the attention she was getting. "You'll meet him tomorrow. And his sister, Haley."

"Great," replied Stacey. "I can't wait. I can't wait to see the other kids, either. I bet they've really changed."

I was about to say that she might not even recognize some of the youngest ones, when I realized that it was 5:35. "Oh! Order!" I cried. "Order! I cannot believe I forgot to bring the meeting to order, and we're five minutes late!"

"Kristy," said Claudia, "it isn't going to kill you."

I knew Claud sounded annoyed because she was still upset, but even so, I replied testily, "Well, I know *that*. But let's get going here. Hmm. No dues to collect. Any club business?"

To my surprise, Stacey said, "Can I ask a question?"

"Of course."

Ring, ring.

"Oops, the phone. Hold on just a sec, Stace."

I was reaching for the phone (so were Mary Anne and Jessi), when Stacey leaped up. "Can I answer it, please? It's been months and months since I've taken a —" (*Ring, ring.*) "— job call here with you guys."

"Sure," the rest of us replied at once.

Stace reached for the phone. "Hello, Baby-sitters Club," she said, sounding like she might either laugh or cry.

(This meeting was emotional for everyone.)

"Doctor Johanssen!" Stacey suddenly exclaimed. "Doctor Johanssen, it's me, Stacey! . . . No, you called Stoneybrook. I'm visiting. I'm here for the weekend. I'm going on the Mother's Day outing tomorrow." (Dr. Johanssen is Charlotte Johanssen's mother, and in case you can't tell, she and Stacey are pretty close. Stacey helped Charlotte through some rough times, and Dr. Johanssen helped Stacey through some rough times.) "Oh, don't tell Charlotte I'm here, okay?" Stacey was saying. "I'll surprise her when she gets to Claudia's tomorrow. . . . Yes. . . . Right. . . . Oh, a sitter for next Saturday? Boy, I wish it could be me. . . . No, I'm leaving the day after tomorrow. But we'll get you a sitter. I'll call right back, okay? . . . Okay. Bye."

Stacey's face went from excited to disappointed and back to excited while Mary Anne looked at our appointment pages. The Johanssen job was for the evening, and we signed Dawn up for it.

Stacey called Charlotte's mother back. While she did, Claud began searching the bedroom.

"What are you looking for?" asked Mal, as if we didn't know. (It must have been junk food.)

"Junk food," Claud replied. "I bought a bag of those licorice strings. I thought we could make jewelry out of them before we ate them. Oh, and Dawn and Stacey, I've got pretzels for you. I know that's not very interesting, but at least the pretzels look like little goldfish."

Claud handed around our snacks.

Then Stacey said, "Um, I had a question . . . ?"

"Oh, right!" I exclaimed. "Sorry, Stace."

"Well, I was just wondering. Could we run through tomorrow's schedule and all the details? I mean, like, who exactly is coming, and if we should expect any problems. I don't even know some of these kids. And you guys have talked about a carnival, but . . ."

"Oh, of course we'll run through everything," spoke up Mary Anne, who was playing with a licorice bracelet. "We didn't mean to leave you out. It's just that *we've* been making plans for so long."

"Anyway, it'll probably help *us* to run through the schedule," added Jessi.

I jumped right in. "I'll start," I said. I try hard not to be bossy, but after all, I *am* the president.

"The kids will come here at eight-thirty," I began. (I was trying to make licorice earrings.) "The fathers have been really cooperative, and they're doing all the stuff like dropping the kids off and picking them up. They're making the lunches, too, and watching any brothers and sisters who are too little —"

"Or too big," added Dawn.

"— to come on the outing. So the moms will really have a day off tomorrow."

"One exception," interrupted Mallory, as she braided together three strings of licorice. "The Barretts."

"Oh, yeah," said Stacey. "No Mr. Barrett."

"Right. So guess what?"

"What, Mal?"

"My dad is going to be Mr. Barrett for the day. He's going to bring Buddy and Suzi with my brother and sisters in the morning and pick them up at the end of the day. He's going to fix their lunches, and he's even going to baby-sit for Marnie all day."

"You are kidding!" cried Stacey.

"Nope. Dad loves little kids. Why do you think there are eight of us?"

We laughed, and I added, "Marnie ought to

spend the day with my mother. It would be, like, a dream come true for Mom."

At that point we almost got off the subject, but I went ahead and outlined the day for Stacey (in between a few job calls).

We were finishing up when Mimi wandered into Claudia's room, and I mean *wandered* in. She looked like someone who had gone for a walk without any destination in mind. She just sauntered in — and then she seemed surprised to find us club members there.

"Oh . . . oh, my," said Mimi vaguely.

Claudia leaped to her feet. "What are you looking for, Mimi?"

"The . . . cow."

The cow? My friends and I glanced at each other. But not one of us was tempted to laugh. This was not funny.

Claudia took her grandmother by the arm and led her gently toward the doorway. On the way, Mimi seemed to "wake up."

"Dinner is almost ready, my Claudia," she said. "To please help salad with me after meeting." (That was normal for Mimi.)

"Sure," agreed Claudia. "Just a few more minutes. Then Stacey and I will come help you."

Mimi left. An awkward silence followed. Jessi tried to make conversation. "I really like your bedroom, Stacey," she began. "You should come over and see it, if you want. The wallpaper is so pretty that we left it up, and my furniture looks great . . ." She trailed off.

Claudia had tears in her eyes again.

Stacey said, "I decided I like it better than my room in New York."

Another awkward silence. Both Mallory and Jessi looked awfully uncomfortable. I wondered if they felt like the new kids on the block all over again.

"I wonder," I said, as if it were the only thing on my mind, "what my mom will look like when she's pregnant."

"Like she's going to tip over," replied Dawn, and we all cracked up. We became ourselves again. In the last few moments of the meeting we giggled and laughed and told school gossip to Stacey. Then the meeting was over. We left Claudia and Stacey, calling to each other, "Bye!" and "See you at eight!" and "Remember your lunches!"

That night, I could barely get to sleep. I was so, so excited about the Mother's Day surprise.

CHAPTER 10

Saturday

I can't believe it. I am actually writing in the Baby-sitters Club notebook! I wasn't sure if this would ever happen again. Mom and Dad made all sorts of promises about letting me come back to Stoneybrook to visit but, well — a club event is almost too good to be true.

Anyway, the morning of the Mother's Day surprise got off to a shaky start. It reminded me of the first day we took care of those fourteen kids at Kristy's. Even though the kids in today's group know each other (mostly) and know us baby-sitters, there are just some children who never like to be left in a new situation. And they let you know by crying . . . .

Well, we did have some tears, but Stacey was right. The morning got off to a shaky start — but not a bad one.

However, the kids' tears came later in the morning. *Stacey* began her day much earlier, waking up in the cot that had been placed in Claudia's room. She yawned and stretched. She looked over at Claudia. Claudia was dead to the world. She could sleep through a tornado. No, a tornado and a hurricane. No, a tornado, a hurricane, a major earthquake, and a garbage truck. Luckily, when Claudia *does* wake up, she gets up fairly easily.

But Stacey didn't need to wake her up right away, which was fine because Stacey wanted to lie in bed and daydream. Actually, what she wanted to do was "rememberize," which was an old word of hers meaning "to remember something really well."

She rememberized the first time she ever met Claudia. It was the beginning of seventh grade — I think it might even have been the first day of school — and they ran into each other in the hallway. I mean, ran *right* into each other. Each of them was kind of mad because the other was dressed in such cool clothes — and each wanted to be *the* coolest. But they calmed down and became very close friends.

Then Stacey rememberized the first time she baby-sat for Charlotte Johanssen. After that, she was about to begin a good daydream about Cam Geary, the gorgeous star, when she realized she really ought to wake up Claudia.

So she did. She leaned across Claud's bed and tapped her on the arm.

"Claud. Hey, Claud!"

"Mmm?"

"Time to get up."

"Why?"

"Mother's Day surprise. The kids'll be here in just a couple of hours."

"Oh!"

Claudia was up in a flash, and she and Stacey got dressed.

Now, here's a big difference between them and me. That morning, I dressed in my jeans and running shoes, a T-shirt with a picture of Beaver Cleaver on it, and my collie dog baseball cap. Then I added my SHS (Stoneybrook High School) sweatshirt that used to belong to Sam, since the weather would probably be chilly in the morning.

Stacey, however, put on a tight-fitting pink jumpsuit over a white T-shirt, lacy white socks, and those plastic shoes. What are they called — jellies? And Claudia wore a pale blue baggy shirt over black-and-blue leopard-spotted pants that tied in neat knots at her ankles. On her feet she wore purple high-tops. And they both wore all this jewelry and these accessories, like big, big earrings, and headbands with rosettes on them, and nail polish. Claudia even wore her snake bracelet. Honestly, what did they think we were going to do? Enter a fashion show?

Oh, okay, I'll admit it. They looked great. And I was a teeny bit jealous. I wouldn't even know *how* to dress the way they do.

Anyway, Stacey and Claudia ate a quick breakfast — they were both kind of nervous — and then waited for the rest of us club members to show up.

"You girls eat like hawks," said Mimi, while they waited.

"She means 'birds,'" Claudia whispered to Stacey.

Stacey nodded.

"What happen today?" Mimi wanted to know. Claud and the rest of the Kishis had only explained this to Mimi about a million times already, but Claudia tried again.

She was halfway finished when the bell rang Stacey ran for the door. She opened it and found — me!

"Hi!" I cried.

"Hi!" replied Stacey. (We were both a little *too* excited.) "You're the first one . . . oh, but here come Jessi and Mallory."

We all arrived before eight o'clock.

"What needs to be done?" asked Stacey nervously.

"Divide up the group tags," I answered.

We had decided that we would color-code our groups. My group was red, Mary Anne's was yellow, Jessi's was green, and so on. It would help the kids to know who they were supposed to be with. It isn't a very good idea to let kids go out in public places wearing name tags, but we figured if, for instance, I was wearing a red tag around my neck, and so were Karen, Andrew, and Shea, at least they'd know the four of us were supposed to stick together.

So at our Wednesday club meeting that week, we'd cut twenty-eight circles out of construction paper and strung them on yarn. They looked like large necklaces. Now we each put one on.

Stacey and I looked at ourselves in a bathroom mirror.

"Ravishing," said Stacey.

I giggled.

"Kristy?" Mal called. "Claud wants you."

"Okay!" I replied.

Stacey and I ran downstairs and found the rest of the club members in the kitchen with Mr. Kishi and Mimi.

"Could you just tell Dad about the lunches again?" Claudia asked me.

"Oh, sure," I said. "All the kids are bringing bag lunches. We're going to leave the lunches here — if it's still okay with you — and then, if you don't mind, could you drive them to Carle Playground at twelve-thirty? We'll meet you there. That way, we won't have to carry the lunches around the carnival all morning. Is that okay with you? We'd really appreciate it."

Mr. Kishi smiled. "It's still just fine. Mimi is going to help me."

But all Mimi said then was, "I've got to get that box over to the planet." She was gazing out the window.

Ordinarily, any one of us club members might have burst into tears then. We were frustrated by

not understanding how Mimi's mind was working these days. We wanted badly to understand.

But the doorbell rang.

"Someone's here!" cried Stacey, leaping to her
feet. "The first kid is here!"

All seven of us sitters raced for the Kishis'
front door.

Not one but six kids were crowded onto the
stoop with their fathers: Jackie, Shea, and Archie
with Mr. Rodowsky, Myriah and Gabbie with Mr.
Perkins, and Jamie with Mr. Newton.

"Hi, you guys!" we greeted them.

Us baby-sitters stepped outside with the color
tags, and the fathers left after kisses and hugs
and good-byes. We thought the kids would feel
more comfortable in the yard, where they could
run around.

I was about to explain the tags to them when
Jamie shrieked, "Stacey!" He ran to her and threw
his arms around her legs. "You came back!"

"Just for a visit," she told him. "Boy, am I glad
to see you! I think you've grown another foot."

Jamie looked down. "Nah. I've still got just
two," he replied, but he was smiling.

"Okay," I said loudly, clapping my hands. "I
have something special for each of you to wear

today." I handed out the tags (Shea Rodowsky said he felt like a *gi-irl*) and then — Becca Ramsey and Charlotte Johanssen arrived.

They were wearing plastic charm bracelets and were so busy comparing the charms that Charlotte didn't see Stacey.

Finally, as Mr. Ramsey was leaving, Stacey stepped up behind Char and tapped her on the shoulder. "Excuse me," she said. "Can you tell me where I could find a Charlotte Johanssen?"

"I'm —" Charlotte started to say. She turned around. She looked up. Her eyes began to widen. They grew and grew and grew. "Stacey!" she managed to say, gasping.

Becca grinned. She was in on the surprise.

"I'm back for the weekend," said Stacey in a wavery voice. Then she knelt down, held her arms open, and Charlotte practically dove into them. Stacey held Charlotte for a long time.

"Yuck," said David Michael, who was watching. He and Karen and Andrew had just arrived.

"Okay, kiddo," I heard Watson say to Andrew. "See you this afternoon. Have a great time at the carnival. I know you'll have fun with Kristy and Karen and David Michael."

Well, even with me there, Andrew was the first of our criers. The next crier was Suzi Barrett.

She looked pretty confused as Mr. Pike dropped her off along with her brother and four of the Pike kids. Then Jenny Prezzioso began to wail. And finally Archie Rodowsky tuned up, even though he'd been fine before.

"Oh, boy," said Stacey.

Two of us took the criers aside and tried to quiet them. They had just calmed down (after all, they knew who we were, where they were, and where they were going), when Mr. Braddock brought Matt and Haley by.

Darn old Jenny Prezzioso let out a squawk. "Is *he* coming?" she exclaimed, pointing to Matt.

Mr. Braddock was leaving — so Haley made a beeline for Jenny.

"You wanna make something of it?" she asked fiercely. "You got a problem with that?" (Haley is a *really* nice kid, but she is super-protective of her brother.)

"No," said Jenny in a small voice. To her credit, she did not start to cry again.

"Kristy," said Stacey, "introduce me to Haley and Matt, okay? Oh, and to Becca. I don't know Jessi's sister."

I nodded. Then I spoke to Jessi. Jessi and Haley introduced Matt to Stacey using sign language. Then Jessi introduced Becca to her.

"I think," I said, "that you know everyone else, Stace. It's pretty much the same crowd."

"Just older," she replied. She smiled ruefully.

"Well, let's get this show on the road!" I said brightly. "Are you kids ready for the carnival?"

"Yes!"

"Are you wearing your tags?"

"Yes!"

"Have you been to the bathroom?"

"Yes." ... "No." ... "I have to go again." ... "Me too." ... "I went at home." ... "I don't *wanna* go."

It took nearly a half an hour for everyone to use the bathroom. When we were ready, we set out for Sudsy's Carnival.

CHAPTER 11

"We're really, really going to the carnival!" exclaimed Jamie Newton, as my friends and I led the twenty-one kids along the sidewalks of Stoneybrook. *"Oh, give me a comb,"* he sang.

I looked around and smiled. The groups were staying together. (So far.) And oddly enough, my funny little group was working out nicely. Because Andrew had cried earlier, Shea was very protective of him. And Karen seemed to have a crush on Shea. She hung onto every word he said, and gazed at him as if he were a superhero. Shea was playing the part of their big brother.

From the other children around me came excited comments:

"I'm going to ride the ferris wheel!"

"Oh, I hope there's a roller coaster!"

"I'm going to win a teddy bear for my sister." (That was Jamie.)

"I wonder what a sideshow is."

"My daddy told me there used to be a circus man named P.T. Barnum, who said there's a sucker born every minute."

"What's that mean?"

A shrug. "Don't know . . . I hope there's cotton candy."

At that point, Stacey turned to me and said, "How are we going to pay for all this? The kids want rides and food and tickets to the sideshow. I don't blame them. I would, too, if I were their age, but . . . this morning is going to be expensive."

"Don't worry," I told her. "First of all, we decided no food at the carnival. We want the kids to eat their own lunches later. Second, we found out how much most of the rides and attractions at Sudsy's will cost and realized that we have enough money for each kid to do three things. And third," (I grinned) "every single kid came with extra money — either part of their allowance, or a little something from one of their parents, so we don't have to —"

"THERE IT IS!"

The shriek came from Jamie, who was at the head of the line with Claudia and the Perkins girls. We had rounded a corner, and in the huge parking lot behind Carle Playground was Sudsy's

Carnival. It spread out before us, a wonderful, confusing mess of rides and booths, colors and smells, people, and even a few animals.

The kids looked overwhelmed, so we walked in slowly, trying to see everything at once. There were a ferris wheel, a merry-go-round, a whip ride, a train, a funhouse, and a spook house. At the midway was a penny pitch, a ring toss, a horserace game, a shooting gallery, and a fish pond for the littlest kids. The sideshow tent was set up at one end of the parking lot, and wandering among the crowds were a man selling oranges with candy straws in them, an organ-grinder with a monkey, and — Jamie's precious clown selling balloons.

"Oh, my gosh," whispered Shea Rodowsky, taking it all in.

Even he was impressed. I took that as a good sign.

Impressive as it was, though, the carnival wasn't all *that* big. I mean, it was just set up in a parking lot. Still, there was plenty to see and do. Us sitters wondered where to start.

The kids solved the problem for us. Karen had spotted the spook house.

"Please, please, please can we go in that haunted house?" she begged.

I hesitated. Would it be too scary? I glanced at my friends and they just shrugged.

What the heck? I thought. How bad could it be?

Sixteen of the kids wanted to walk through the haunted house. (Andrew, Archie Rodowsky, Suzi Barrett, and Gabbie Perkins were too young, and prissy Jenny announced that the house would probably be filthy dirty.) So Mary Anne stayed outside with them (she looked relieved), and the rest of us paid for our tickets and filed into the house.

"Where are the cars?" asked Karen. "What do we ride in?"

Not long ago, we had been to Disney World in Florida. We went on this incredible ride through a haunted mansion.

But that was Disney World, this was Sudsy's.

"You just walk through this house, Karen," I told her.

Karen looked disappointed, until we turned the first dark corner — and a ghost suddenly lit up before us. Shea, Buddy Barrett, Nicky Pike, and David Michael burst out laughing. A few kids gasped. Karen shrieked.

"It's all right," I told her, taking her hand.

We passed through the Death Chamber. "Cobwebs" swept over our faces. "Thunder" roared overhead. And a very realistic-looking bolt of lightning zigzagged to the floor with a crackle and a crash.

"Let me out!" cried Karen, as a headless ghost floated by. "Let me out!"

"Karen, I can't. We're in the middle of the spook house. We have to keep going. There's no other way out."

"Oh, yes there is," said an eerie voice.

I almost screamed myself before I realized that the voice sounded weird because it was coming from behind a mask.

"I work here," said a person dressed as a mummy. "There are exits all over the place. I can let you out if you want."

"Karen?" I asked.

"Yes, please," she replied, shivering.

I tapped Claudia, who happened to be standing right behind me, and told her that Karen and I were leaving. "The rest of you will have to watch the kids. Karen and I will meet you at that bench near Mary Anne."

"No problem," replied Claudia.

The groups were all mixed up, but it didn't seem to matter.

The mummy discreetly opened a door in a pitch-black wall, and Karen and I followed them into the bright sunshine.

"Whew," said Karen.

The mummy removed his mask. He was a she.

"Thank you so much," I said. "I guess we were a little panicky." I was trying not to lay all the blame on Karen.

Karen looked at her feet in embarrassment anyway.

The mummy smiled. "My name's Barbara," she said. "And don't feel bad. At least once a day, someone needs to use one of the special exit doors." She knelt in front of Karen. "I'll tell you some secrets," she said.

Tell Karen secrets? That was like telling secrets to the National Broadcasting Company.

"I'll tell you how they do the special effects," Barbara went on, "but you have to promise never to reveal the secrets."

Oh, brother, I thought. All of Stoneybrook would know within a week.

By the time we reached Mary Anne, the other kids were emerging from the haunted house. They were excited, and so was Karen, who was bursting with her precious knowledge.

"Rides! Rides! Let's go on rides!" chanted Vanessa Pike.

The chant was taken up by the other kids, so we set out across the parking lot. Before we were halfway there we were stopped by —

"The balloon-seller!" exclaimed Jamie.

Only he turned out to be a balloon-giver. The clown handed a free Sudsy's Carnival helium balloon to each kid. Then he walked away.

"What a nice man," said Suzi Barrett.

Us sitters began tying the balloons to the kids' wrists and our own. Just before Mallory could tackle Jackie Rodowsky's, it slipped out of his hand and floated away.

"Oh, Jackie," cried Mallory in dismay, even though he *is* our walking disaster. We know to expect these things.

But Jackie didn't look the least bit upset. "My balloon is on its way to the moon, you know," he said. "That's where these things go." He indicated the colorful garden of helium balloons around him.

"They go to the moon?" repeated Nina Marshall.

In a flash, the kids were slipping the balloons off their wrists.

"My balloon is going to the moon, too," said Claire Pike.

"Yeah," agreed Myriah Perkins.

"Not mine," said Jamie firmly. "Mine is for Lucy." He held out his wrist so Claudia could tie his balloon to it securely.

Balloonless (or almost balloonless) we reached the rides. Suddenly, my friends and I could hear nothing but, "I'm going on the whip," or, "I hope we get stuck at the top of the ferris wheel," or, "Look, Gabbie, a train."

I smiled. I kept smiling until I heard a voice say, "*Please* let me go on the whip with you, Nicky."

"No way," he replied.

"No way is right, Margo." I looked around for Mallory. "Mal," I said urgently, running over to her and her purple group, "Margo wants to go on the whip."

"No. Oh, no."

Margo is famous for her motion sickness. She gets airsick, carsick, seasick, you name it. So you can see why the whip was not a good idea.

Mallory ran to her sister. "Margo," she said in a no-nonsense voice, "you can't go on any rides."

Margo's face puckered up. "But everyone else

is going on something. Even the little kids are going to ride on the train."

The train was pretty lame. All it did was travel slowly around a track in a circle. The kids sat in the cars and rang bells.

"Hey," said Mallory, "you could go on the train, Margo. That wouldn't make you sick. At least, I don't think so."

"The train is for babies!" cried Margo, looking offended.

Mallory and her sister watched the rest of us kids and sitters line up for the rides we'd chosen. At last Mal said, "We-ell . . . maybe you could ride the merry-go-round, Margo. You can sit on one of those fancy benches. I don't want you on a horse that goes up and down."

"All right," agreed Margo, brightening.

Mallory accompanied her sister on the carousel. They sat on a red-and-gold bench. The music started. The ride began. It went faster and faster until —

"Mallory," said Margo suddenly, "I'm dizzy. I don't feel too good."

The words were barely out of her mouth before Margo's breakfast was all over the floor of the merry-go-round.

The Sudsy's people were not too happy. Neither was Stacey, who had seen the whole thing and can't stand the sight of barf.

It was time for quieter activities. We left the rides. Some of the kids played games and won prizes. Jamie tried desperately to win a teddy bear for Lucy, but all he could get was a squirt gun.

The younger kids had their faces made up.

Mallory and Margo sat in the first-aid tent.

Jessi's group peeked into the sideshow tent and decided it looked like a rip-off.

By 12:15, half of the kids were begging for cotton candy and popcorn, so we left Sudsy's. It was on to Carle Playground for lunch.

CHAPTER 12

"But . . . but . . . box is not at planet. No, I mean *is* at planet, but where are my forks? And TV people. I try to watch *Wheel of Fortune*, and TV people are bother me. Will not leave alone."

I glanced at Claudia. My friends and I and the children had just reached Carle Playground, and there were Mr. Kishi, Mimi, and our lunches.

And as you must have guessed by now, Mimi was having some trouble again. I think it was because she wasn't quite sure why she was at a playground with her son-in-law, her granddaughter, her granddaughter's friends, twenty-one children, and twenty-eight lunches. It could confuse anybody.

I gave Mimi a kiss and told her not to worry about the TV people.

Mimi flashed me an odd look. "TV people? What TV people? We have lunch to hand out. Better begin. Big job. Where is my Claudia?"

Mimi fades in and out.

I located Claudia. Then Mr. Kishi, Mimi, and my friends and I handed out the lunches. Very reluctantly, I put Margo's in her hands.

"How are you feeling?" I asked her, as she climbed onto a bench between her sisters.

"Hungry?" she replied, as if she didn't expect me to believe her.

"Really?"

"Honest."

"Okay," I said doubtfully. "But eat very, very slowly."

Margo nodded seriously. "I will."

Mr. Kishi and Mimi slid into the car then and drove back to their house.

The twenty-eight of us sat down and began eating right away. (We were starving.) We took up three entire picnic tables. I looked at my red group. Andrew, with a purple juice mustache, was munching away at his tuna-fish sandwich. Shea, a doughnut in one hand and an apple in the other, was watching Andrew fondly.

"I bet you're going to eat that whole sandwich, aren't you?" he said to Andrew. "That's really great. If you do, you might get muscles as big as Popeye's."

And Karen was just gazing adoringly at Shea. At one point she said, "You know how they —"

but she clapped her hand over her mouth. I knew she had almost given away one of the secrets she learned at the spook house. I'm sure she thought it would be a really terrific "gift" for Shea.

Up and down my table and even at the other tables, I could hear various comments and see various kinds of eating going on. For example:

Jenny Prezzioso is a slow, picky eater. She ate almost everything that was in her bag, but she did it in her own way. First she nibbled the crusts off of her sandwiches. "Okay. All tidy," she said to herself. Then she ate the insides of the sandwiches in rows. When she had two strips left, one from each sandwich half, she began playing with them. (I think she was getting full.) She played with them until they were dirty and had to be thrown out.

Jackie Rodowsky, our lovable walking disaster, dropped everything at least once. He was like a cartoon character. Accidentally (it's *always* an accident with Jackie), he flipped his fork to the ground. As he picked it up, he knocked his orange off the paper plate it was resting on. He returned the orange, knocked the fork off again, picked it up, spilled his Coke, and while trying to mop up the Coke in his lap, knocked his fork to the ground again.

Mary Anne, sitting across the table from him, nearly turned purple trying not to laugh.

Another kid I liked to watch was Buddy Barrett. He was the last person on earth I would have expected to be picky — but he was picky. He examined nearly every bite before putting it in his mouth.

"This has," he said, frowning, "a black speck. Look, right there." He leaned across the table to show it to Nicky Pike.

"So pick it off," said Nicky, who would probably eat something that had been rolling around in a mud puddle.

Buddy picked it off and gingerly ate the rest of the bite of sandwich.

Then there were Myriah and Gabbie, who were nibbling their sandwiches into shapes — a bunny, a cat face, a snowman, and a dinosaur.

Shea ate everything practically without chewing it. He just wolfed things down — an apple, a sandwich, a bag of Fritos. He finished his entire lunch before Margo Pike ate a quarter of her sandwich.

"Margo?" asked Mallory. "Are you feeling okay?"

Margo nodded. "I'm just eating slowly. Kristy said to."

I glanced at Mallory and shrugged. I hadn't meant for Margo to eat like a snail, but I guessed it couldn't hurt an upset stomach.

Fwwwt. Nicky Pike blew a straw paper at Matt Braddock. Matt grinned, grabbed a straw from his sister, blew the paper at Nicky, then returned the opened straw to Haley.

Haley signed, "Very funny," to Matt.

Matt signed back, "I know."

Suddenly from the end of one table, I heard the beginnings of a song that I knew could lead to trouble — the hysterical kind of trouble in which a kid may laugh so hard he won't be able to finish his lunch. Or worse, he'll lose his lunch.

David Michael, my own brother, was singing. (I should have known.)

"The Addams Family started," he began.

Andrew giggled, knowing what was coming.

"When Uncle Fester farted."

Shea Rodowsky choked on his Twinkie, then laughed. And Haley Braddock laughed so hard she sprayed apple juice out of her nose.

"Oh, lord," said Claudia, looking at Haley. "What a mess."

We cleaned up Haley and her apple juice. Then we cleaned up straw papers and napkins and plastic forks.

"If you guys are done," I announced to the kids, "please put your thermoses and things back in your bags or lunch boxes. Anyone who's finished can go play. *Quietly*, since you just ate."

A sea of kids rose from the picnic tables. The only one left was Margo Pike. She was now eating the second quarter of her sandwich.

Stacey looked at her oddly. But before she could say a word, Margo said, "I'm eating slowly, *okay*?" She acted as if she'd been asked that question seventy-five times.

So while Margo ate, the rest of the kids explored the playground.

"Look! Horsies!" Nina Marshall called to Gabbie Perkins and Jamie Newton. She had found three of those horses on springs. They were painted like the horses we'd seen on the merry-go-round at the carnival.

"Go easy!" Claudia called to them.

The older boys found a much better activity. Shea started it. Our groups were completely mixed up again (which was okay, since everyone seemed to be getting along) and Shea, Jackie, David Michael, Buddy, Nicky, and Matt were gathered around two water fountains that were facing each other.

"Hey!" said Shea. "Look!" He turned the water

on, then held his thumb over the stream of water, which sent it in an arc to the other fountain.

"Cool!" cried Nicky. He tried the trick with the second fountain and sent the water to the first one.

"Oh, I am so thirsty," signed Buddy to Matt. He stood by one fountain, opened his mouth, and Matt, catching on, sent a stream of water from the other fountain right into Buddy's mouth.

"Whoa, do I ever have an idea," said Nicky. "But I have to go get Claire. I'll be right back." Nicky went in search of his littlest sister.

He found Margo at the picnic table. "What are you doing?" he asked her.

"Still eating," she replied with clenched teeth. She took a teensy bite out of a plum.

"Well, where's Claire?"

Margo pointed to the slide, where Claire was whooshing down headfirst on her tummy. She stopped at the end and leapt to her feet like a gymnast.

"Hey, Claire! Come here!" called Nicky.

"Why?" asked Claire warily.

"Just come."

Claire followed him reluctantly to the water fountains.

"Stand here," Nicky directed her.

Claire stood between the fountains.

Nicky poised himself at one fountain. Buddy was at the other.

"Now!" cried Nicky.

Claire was hit by streams of cold water on both sides of her face.

Jessi went running to the water fountains. "Nicky! Buddy!" she began.

But before she could get any further, Claire burst out laughing. Water soaked her hair and dripped down her face, but she giggled and exclaimed, "Do it again!"

The boys, sure they were in trouble, looked at Jessi.

"Once," said Jessi. "You may do it once more. Then leave the water fountains alone."

The boys sprayed Claire, and she practically fainted from laughter. Jessi smiled but ushered everyone away.

Margo sat at the table, putting crumb-sized bites of graham cracker in her mouth.

Nina, Gabbie, and Jamie rocked on the horses.

By the swings, a small group of kids was gathering. Karen was at the center of them. They were very quiet — except for Karen. I glanced at Dawn. "I better see what Karen's up to," I said.

I crept toward the group until I could hear

Karen say, "And they use masks to make the awful —"

Karen looked up and saw me. I raised my eyebrows at her.

"To — to, um, make the . . . Oh, it isn't impor — My gosh, look at that!" she exclaimed.

Eight faces turned to see a robin sitting in an ash tree.

"Big deal," said David Michael.

"I've seen a thousand robins," added Haley Braddock.

"Yeah!" called Margo, still at the picnic table. She took a tiny bite out of her plum, most of which was still uneaten.

"Boy, are you a slowpoke," said Jenny, running to Margo.

"She is not!" cried Claire, rushing to defend her sister. "She was sick."

"She's still slow."

"Is not!"

"Is too!"

Claire rushed at Jenny, but Mary Anne ran between them, just in time to ward off a fight.

At that moment, Andrew tripped, fell, and skinned both knees. He burst into tears.

"You guys!" I said to the other sitters. "I think it's time to go to Claudia's. We all need a rest."

CHAPTER 13

Well, I think today went pretty well.
Really. I mean, so there were a few
scrapes and arguments. We were taking
care of twenty-one children. What did we
expect? (With seven brothers and sisters,
you learn to "go with the flow," as my
mom would say.) I think one upset stomach,
one set of skinned knees, one argument,
and a practical joke are pretty good.

Anyway, after Andrew fell, and Jenny
and Claire had been separated, we left
the playground. My group — Buddy, David
Michael, and Jackie — was in fine shape.
They'd had a great day so far. They'd
been to the carnival, walked through a
spook houses, flown balloons to the moon,

ridden the whip, won some prizes,
and discovered the greatest water
fountains of all time.

A few other kids weren't quite so
happy, though.

That's true. Mallory's group was in fine shape, while a few others weren't, but it wasn't any big deal. Everything was under control.

Us baby-sitters helped the kids collect their things — lunch boxes and thermoses, plus souvenirs from the carnival. Jamie tucked his squirt gun into his lunch box. Suzi was wearing a hat that made her look like the Statue of Liberty. Myriah was wearing a plastic necklace, and Gabbie was wearing a red bracelet that said *Sudsy's* on it.

"WAHHH!" cried Andrew as we walked away from the playgound. We'd washed his knees at the water fountain, using clean napkins, but they did look a little painful.

"We can get some Band-Aids at Claudia's," Mallory said to me.

Andrew wasn't the only one crying.

"WAHHH!" wailed Jenny and Claire.

"Keep them apart," Mallory whispered to Mary Anne. "I'm not kidding. They get along okay most of the time, but when they're mad, well . . ."

I almost expected Mal to say, "It's not a pretty sight."

Anyway, poor Mary Anne had her hands full between trying to separate Claire and Jenny, and keeping her eye on Margo and her touchy stomach.

Mallory saved the day, though. We'd just reached the edge of the playground and our criers were still crying. Jamie was starting to get mad about not having won a teddy bear for Lucy (even though he had a balloon for her), and Nicky and Buddy were walking behind Vanessa, trying to see if they could touch her hair without her noticing.

Trouble was brewing.

So suddenly Mallory let loose with, *"The ants go marching one by one —"*

"Hurrah! Hurrah!" chimed in Nicky and Mal's sisters.

"The ants go marching one by one —"

"Hurrah! Hurrah!"

"The ants go marching one by one," sang Mal, *"the little one stops to suck his thumb, and they all go marching down . . . beneath . . . the earth."*

Most of the kids were looking at the Pikes with interest. The criers had stopped crying. The complainers had stopped complaining. The teasers had stopped teasing.

So the song continued. The kids didn't know it, but they chimed in when they could. They always had to stop singing to find out what the little one did, though. (Two by two, he has to stop to tie his shoe. Three by three, he falls and skins his knee.) The song occupied the kids all the way to Claudia's house, by which time we were pretty glad to hear it end. Mallory knew only twelve verses, and we heard each of them a number of times.

"Just be glad it wasn't 'Ninety-Nine Bottles of Beer on the Wall,'" said Stacey, looking pale.

"Shh!" I hissed. "One of the kids might hear you."

At Claudia's, us sitters went into action.

I took Andrew into the Kishis' bathroom, washed his knees again, put some first aid cream on them, and then applied a fat Band-Aid to each one. Andrew liked the Band-Aids a lot.

"I feel better already!" he announced.

By the time we were outside again, things were going so smoothly I was amazed. The kids — all of them — were gathered under a tree with Mallory, Stacey, and Jessi, who were singing with them while the rest of us sitters got organized.

I kept hearing snatches of song, most of them sung by Mallory.

I heard: *"I've got sixpence, jolly, jolly sixpence. I've got sixpence to last me all my life . . ."*

Then I heard: *"Oh, we ain't got a barrel of money. Maybe we're ragged and funny . . ."*

And then: *"Won't you come home, Bill Bailey? Won't you come home?"*

(Where does Mal learn all this stuff?)

Finally I heard Jessi and Stacey teach the kids a round: *"Heigh-ho, nobody at home. Meat nor drink nor money have I none. Yet will I be me-e-e-e-erry. Heigh-ho, nobody at home."*

The round sort of got lost because the kids were saying things like, *"Heigh-ho, no one's at my house."* But you could get the gist of it.

Anyway, while the kids were singing, Dawn, the world's most organized person, took their bags, thermoses, lunch boxes, prizes, and extra sweaters, and organized them under a tree. When the fathers arrived to pick up their kids, nothing would be missing or hard to locate. Meanwhile, Claudia had found her art materials and was setting them out on the Kishis' picnic tables. And

Mary Anne had found the stack of books we'd borrowed from the library.

"Okay!" I called as another round of "Heigh-Ho" came to an end. "Who wants to make a Mother's Day card?"

"Me!" cried all twenty-one kids.

"Great," I replied. "Everyone will get a turn, but half of you will read stories with Mallory and Jessi and me first. Then we'll switch."

Well, *that* was not the way to present things, because all the kids wanted to go first, but at last we got the problem sorted out. Live and learn.

Mal and I read *Where the Wild Things Are* and *One Morning in Maine* and *The Cat in the Hat* to the younger children, while Jessi read *If I Ran the Circus* and a chapter from a Paddington book to the older kids.

Then it was time for the children to trade places. The ones who had just made cards brought them over to Mal and Jessi and me. They were very proud of them.

"Look," said Claire. "Look at my card."

I looked. It said, "HAPPY MOTH'S DAY LOVE CLAIRE."

Shea held his out shyly. On the front was written, "Dear Mom, you are . . ." and inside was written:

```
Marvelous
Outstanding
Tops
Honored
Excellent
Renowned
```

Jackie's was covered with smudges and drops of glue, with splotches and mistakes. It read: "Daer Mom, I love you. Love, Your sun, Jackie Rodowsky."

"Beautiful, Jackie," I told him, and he beamed.

The stories began again. The card-making began again. And before we knew it, Myriah Perkins was calling, "Hey, there's Daddy!"

And there he was. He was followed by Mr. Pike and Mr. Prezzioso. The kids started to gather their things. The littlest ones ran to their fathers and threw their arms around them.

Our day was over. The Mother's Day surprise was over. I felt sort of sad. But glad, too, because it had gone so well. I listened to the kids chattering away: "Daddy! I went on a ride. Let's tell Mommy!" said Jenny. And, "I have to tell Mommy about the balloon man," said Jamie. And, "We found the neatest water fountains," exclaimed Nicky. And, "Daddy, I threw up on the merry-go-round," said you-know-who.

"Oh," replied Mr. Pike, "Mommy will love to hear that."

CHAPTER 14

"**W**ell?" I said.

"Well what?" replied Claudia.

The children were gone. Except for Andrew, Karen, and David Michael. They and I were at the Kishis' waiting for Charlie to pick us up and take us home. The rest of the sitters were still at Claud's, too. We had cleaned up every last crayon and shred of paper, but we just couldn't bear to part. So while my little sister and brothers sat under a tree and looked at the library books, the members of the Baby-sitters Club lolled around on the Kishis' porch.

"Well what?" said Claudia again.

"Well, what did everyone decide about Mother's Day presents?" I asked, not daring even to glance at Mary Anne. "Was the Mother's Day surprise good enough?"

"I'll say," said Mal. "It turned out better than

I'd hoped. I bet it was the best Mother's Day present Mom ever got. Especially when Dad pitched in."

"Ditto," said Jessi.

"Ditto," I said. "Mom got to spend the day alone with Watson, since Sam and Charlie went to school to help at a car wash to raise money for the football team."

"And our homemade presents are finished," announced Dawn.

"Well, they are, except for mine," said Stacey. "But Claudia's helping me, so I'll be done tonight."

"What did you make?" I asked.

Claudia, Stacey, and Dawn exchanged grins.

"Personalized pins," replied Claud. "My idea," she added proudly.

"They're more like brooches, though," said Stace.

"What do you mean, personalized pins?" asked Jessi.

"See," said Claud, "we went to the miniatures store and bought things that are meaningful to our mothers. . . . Well, I had to get Stacey's things for her since she wasn't here."

"Yeah," agreed Stacey, "and she did a good job. Like, my mom can sew, and she likes to travel and read, and she likes dogs even though we don't have one. So Claudia bought a tiny airplane, book, thimble, pair of scissors, and dog."

"And then," Dawn continued, "we mixed up the little charms with glass beads and colored flowers, and we glued everything to a metal piece with a pin attached —"

"You can get those things at the crafts store," added Claudia.

"— and, ta-dah! A brooch. Each one different. Just for our mothers."

"Great idea!" I exclaimed.

"I, um, made a decision. I mean about Mother's Day," said Mary Anne.

Six heads swiveled toward her.

"I'm giving my father a Mother's Day present. He's been a good father *and* a good mother to me, or at least he's tried to be, and I want to let him know it."

"Mary Anne! That's great!" I cried. "We never thought of giving your *dad* a *Mother's* Day present."

The others were smiling, so Mary Anne began to smile, too. "You don't think it's corny?" she asked.

"No way!" exclaimed Mallory.

"What did you get him?" asked Jessi.

"A book. It's not very original, but it's hard to

126

know what to get him. And I have to give him stuff on his birthday and Christmas and of course Father's Day, too. So I can't always be original. Anyway, I know he wants this book."

Beep, beep!

Charlie had pulled into the Kishis' driveway. Sam was next to him in the front seat. The car was sparkling clean. I figured they'd taken it through the car wash. Mom and Watson would be happy. The money had gone to a good cause, *and* the station wagon was clean.

"Come on, you guys!" I called to Andrew, David Michael, and Karen.

I said good-bye to my friends. Then my sister and brothers and I squished into the backseat, and Charlie drove home.

The six of us entered our house (okay, our mansion), bursting with news and stories. But we stopped in our tracks when we reached the living room. No kidding. We came to a dead halt.

There were Mom and Watson standing next to each other, very formally, their arms linked. They looked nervous, happy, and surprised all at the same time.

Karen and my brothers and I glanced from our parents to each other, then back to our parents. Not one of us said a word.

After a few moments, Watson cleared his throat. Then Mom cleared *her* throat. Mom was the one who finally spoke.

"Watson and I have some wonderful news," she said. "We just heard it this afternoon. Let's sit down."

So we did. I sat on the floor, leaning against a couch. Andrew sat in my lap. Karen sat beside me, her head resting on my shoulder. My brothers lined up on the couch behind us. We knew this was good news — but not like we'd just bought another TV or something. This sounded like life-changing news.

(I was pretty sure Mom was finally pregnant.)

"Hey, Mom, are you pregnant?" asked Sam for the four-thousandth time.

"No," she replied, "but we've adopted a child."

Adopted a child! Well, that was a different story!

"You've *what*?" cried Charlie.

"We've adopted a little girl, Emily Michelle," said Watson. "She's two years old and she's from Vietnam."

"We'll pick her up at the airport tomorrow," added Mom. "And then she'll be ours."

"We wanted to tell you about this before," said Watson. "It's been in the works for so long. But we didn't want to say a word until we knew something for sure. Things kept falling through. This is definite, though."

Andrew stirred in my lap, and I knew he didn't really understand what was happening.

"So," said my mother nervously, "what does everybody think?"

What did we think? What did *I* think?

"I think . . ." I said, "I think this is totally fantastic!"

Suddenly I was so excited I could barely contain myself. A baby (sort of). Furthermore, I was getting another sister! I'd always thought there weren't enough girls in my family. Before Mom married Watson, it was me against three brothers. After the wedding, it was Karen and me against four brothers. Emily Michelle Thomas Brewer would almost even things up.

But it was more than that, of course. Even more than the stuff about Mom and Watson. I love kids. And we were adopting a two-year-old girl. She would be somebody to dress and play with. She would be somebody to teach things to. Things like, a family is just a group of people who love each other, whether they're brothers and sisters and parents, or stepbrothers and stepsisters and stepparents. Or adopted kids.

Sam and Charlie were as excited as I was.

"This," said Sam, "is really cool." He grinned.

"I can't wait to teach her how to play baseball," added Charlie.

"Hey, that'll be my job!" I cried.

David Michael seemed less certain. "Do two-year-olds wear diapers?" he wanted to know.

"Some of them do," answered Mom.

"Well, I'm not touching those Huggies things. Dirty or clean. But I guess a little sister will be okay. I mean, I've already got one," he said, poking Karen's back with his toe. "And she hasn't killed me yet."

Karen turned around and stuck her tongue out at David Michael.

"Karen?" said Watson. "What about you?"

"What about me?" Karen knew what her father meant, but she was being difficult. After a pause she sighed and said, "I thought *I* was your little girl."

Watson looked thoughtful. "You're one of them. Kristy's my little girl, too."

I didn't complain about being called a little girl. I knew that Watson was trying to make a point.

"Think of it, Karen," I said. "She's only two. Practically a baby. You can help her with things.

You'll be her big sister. You can show her how to play with toys, you can teach her to color, and you can dress her up. It'll be fun!"

Karen smiled, despite herself. "Yeah . . ." she said slowly.

"Andrew?" said Watson. "What do you think?"

"*Whose* baby is she?" asked Andrew. "Why is she coming to our house?"

Oops. I guess we had some explaining to do.

Watson took care of the explaining while Mom and the rest of us did other things.

Boy, was there a lot to do. "We have to get a room ready for Emily," said Mom. And suddenly I remembered my mother talking about our spare bedrooms.

"A room!" I said. "What about clothes? What about toys?"

"I think we have plenty of toys here for now," said Mom. "We can buy some things for a younger child later."

"Well, we don't have any clothes for two-year-olds," I pointed out.

"She'll have a few things of her own, honey," Mom said patiently. "I'll buy her more on Monday. I think the room is the most important project to tackle now. She needs a place of her own from the beginning."

"Wait a sec," I said. "You'll buy her clothes on Monday? On Monday you'll be at work. So will Watson. The rest of us will be in school. What are we going to do with Emily all day?"

Mom was bustling upstairs and I followed her. "Watson and I are taking some time off from our jobs to be with Emily," she said. "We're going to find a nanny while we're at it."

A nanny? Like Mary Poppins? Boy, were things changing. I wondered if a nanny would make my bed for me.

We started in on Emily's room, all eight of us. We chose a room that was near Mom and Watson's. Some furniture was in it already, but it looked like an old lady's room. We got toys and a crib out of the attic, and put some pictures on the wall. The room began to improve. A rocking chair helped. So did a white bookshelf and an old Mother Goose lamp.

"Not bad," I said. I still couldn't believe that the next day I would have a new sister.

Andrew looked up at me. We were alone in the room while everyone else was in the basement, searching for a particular dresser. I was supposed to be arranging David Michael's old picture books on the shelf.

"It is so bad," wailed Andrew, and he began to cry. His cry wasn't one of those Kristy-I-skinned-my-knees-and-want-Band-Aids-the-size-of-dinosaur cries. It was a Kristy-I'm-very-confused-and-a-little-afraid cry.

I knelt down and drew him to me. "Whatever happens, you know," I told him, "you're still going to be our Andrew."

That night, I called every single member of the Baby-sitters Club to tell them the news. I was so excited, I didn't know how I was going to wait until the next day for Emily to arrive. But making five phone calls helped pass the time. I would say to each of my friends, "I'm going to have a new sister!"

And whomever I was talking to would say, "Oh, your mom's going to have a baby! That's great!"

And then I would tell my news. Each time I did, the person on the other end would have to shriek and scream for a few seconds. Then she would ask lots of questions. I was glad for that, because by the time I got into bed, I was exhausted and knew I would be able to sleep.

CHAPTER 15

I slept okay that night, but I was up at six o'clock the next morning. I don't know the last time I voluntarily got up at that hour on a weekend. But who can sleep on the day her sister is arriving? Not I.

I tiptoed downstairs and found that I wasn't the first one awake. Mom and Watson were sitting at the kitchen table, sipping coffee. A high chair had been placed at one end of the table.

"Morning, Watson," I said. Then, "Hi, Mom. Happy Mother's Day!" I kissed her cheek.

"Thanks, honey."

"I wish I had a present for you, but you got your gift yesterday."

"Oh, I know," replied Mom enthusiastically. "And it was great."

"Funny," I said. "We called yesterday's outing the Mother's Day surprise. But I think Emily is the *real* Mother's Day surprise. At least she is to me."

"In a way she is to us, too," spoke up Watson, as I slid into my chair with a glass of orange juice. "We've been trying to adopt for quite awhile. It takes time. We feel lucky to have Emily at last."

"Mom? Watson?" I asked. "How come you adopted? You could have had a kid of your own, couldn't you?"

"Yes," said my mother, "we could have. But I've already given birth to four children."

"And I've got two," added Watson.

"So we decided not to create a seventh. We decided to find a child who's already here but who needs a home. And when we went looking, we finally found Emily."

I nodded. "I like that . . . Boy, is it weird to see all this baby stuff." The high chair was at the table, a stroller was parked by the back door, and a car seat was waiting to be taken into the garage.

Mom and Watson smiled, looking like proud new parents.

They left for the airport around noon.

When Sam, Charlie, and I told them we weren't going to leave the house — we wanted to be here for the very first glimpse of Emily — us kids were left in charge of each other.

As soon as Watson's car left the garage, I looked at my sister and brothers. "What are we going to do now?" I asked them.

We made about a thousand suggestions — and turned them down. At last I said, "I know what we're going to do. Well, I know what *I'm* going to do."

"What?" asked Sam and Charlie.

"Invite the Baby-sitters Club over." That would be great. Even Stacey could come. She wasn't leaving for New York until much later in the afternoon.

"Oh, no, no. Please, no!" moaned Sam.

"All those *girls*?" added David Michael.

I made a face at him. "You know all those girls. You spent yesterday with them."

"*I* didn't," said Sam. "I don't want them here."

"I thought you liked girls so much."

"I like the girls in my class. If you invite your friends over, it's going to be like a slumber party here."

"Oh, it is not," I replied, reaching for the phone.

"Besides, what's wrong with girls?" asked Karen.

My friends showed up within an hour. Each time the doorbell rang, Sam and David Michael pretended to faint. But I have to admit that Sam was pretty impressed when Stacey immediately suggested a good project for the afternoon.

"We should welcome Emily," she said. "We should bake her a cake or something."

"Make a sign," added Sam, brightening.

"How about cookies instead of a cake?" said Mal. "She's only two. She might like cookies better."

"Okay," I agreed.

"From scratch, or those slice-and-bake things?" asked Charlie.

"Scratch," I replied immediately. "That'll take longer, and we want to fill up the whole afternoon. If we need any ingredients, you can run to the store."

"Oh, thanks," said Charlie, but I could tell he didn't really mind, as long as he was here when Emily came home.

"How come I don't get cookies?" asked Andrew, clinging to my legs. "Did anyone bake cookies for me when I was born?"

"I don't know," I replied honestly. What I did know was that Andrew didn't really want answers to his questions. He wanted a hug. So I gave him one.

It turned out that we had all the ingredients

for chocolate chip cookies. We also had paper, scissors, string, and crayons for making a WELCOME EMILY sign. We divided up the jobs. Stacey, Claudia, Mary Anne, Jessi, Sam, and David Michael covered the dining room table with newspaper and went to work on the sign. The rest of us began making a triple batch of cookies. Except for Andrew. He wandered back and forth between the projects, occasionally whining. He couldn't seem to settle down.

I stood at the table next to Dawn, who was stirring the cookie batter. She was humming a vaguely familiar song under her breath.

"What *is* that song?" asked Charlie.

"It's — You know, it goes, *'Lucy in the sky-y with di-i-amonds'.*"

"Oh," said, Charlie. "That old one."

Dawn nodded. She continued singing it softly. *". . . the girl with colitis goes by."*

"What?" I said.

"What?!" cried Sam. He let out a guffaw.

Dawn looked puzzled.

"It's *'the girl with kaleidoscope eyes',*" he informed her.

Dawn and I glanced at each other and shrugged.

"Either way it's a weird song," I said.

We finished our cookies. The sign-makers finished their sign.

"Did someone make me a sign when I was born?" asked Andrew.

I hugged him again. Then I sat down and pulled him onto my lap. "I will always love you," I whispered into his ear. "No matter what. Even if we adopt sixteen more kids, I will always love you because you're Andrew. And so will Karen and your daddy and my mom and David Michael and Sam and Charlie and everyone else."

Andrew smiled a tiny smile. He looked relieved.

"Where should we put the sign?" asked Claudia.

We ended up stringing it across the kitchen. (We were pretty sure Mom and Watson would bring Emily in through the door from the garage to the kitchen.)

Then we piled the cookies into a neat mound on a platter and set the platter on the kitchen table.

"Well, now what?" asked Sam.

"Now," I began. I paused. "They're here! They're *here!*" I screeched. "I heard the car pull into the garage! I swear I did!"

"Oh, lord!" cried Claudia.

"What should we do? What should we *do*?" Mary Anne was wringing her hands.

"Let's stand under the sign," I suggested, "next to the cookies."

We posed ourselves — the six Thomas and Brewer kids in the front, and my friends in the back, even though Mary Anne didn't show up because she's short and was standing behind Charlie.

We were ready. Emily's first sight when she came into her new home, would be of her special sign, her welcome-home cookies, and her brothers and sisters and friends.

The door opened. Mom came in first. Watson was behind her. He was carrying Emily Michelle Thomas Brewer in his arms.

She was fast asleep.

Mom looked at the sign and the cookies and then at Emily. I could tell she felt bad for us. But *we* didn't feel *too* bad. Emily would see everything later.

Mom put her finger to her lips, and we all crowded silently around Emily. I knew we wanted to say things like, "Ooh, look!" Or, "She's so *cute!*" Or, "I can't believe she's my sister!" But we just stared.

Emily's hair is dark and shiny. It falls across her forehead in bangs. Her skin is smooth, and her mouth and nose are tiny, like any two-year-old's. I wished I could see her eyes. You can tell a lot about a person by looking at her eyes.

Emily Michelle. She's my sister, and David Michael's and Sam's and Charlie's. She's Andrew's and Karen's. She's the one person in our family who isn't a Brewer or a Thomas. Her mother is Mom and her father is Watson, but she isn't *their* baby; if you know what I mean.

She's just *ours*. She belongs to Watson and Andrew and Karen, and she belongs to Mom and my brothers and me.

Mom made motions to let us know that she and Watson were going to take Emily upstairs to her crib. I nodded. Charlie and I followed. The others stayed behind. They could see Emily later.

Charlie and I stood in the doorway to Emily's room. We watched Watson lay our new sister in her crib. We watched Mom take Emily's shoes off, then cover her with a blanket. Emily stirred and made a soft, sleepy noise but didn't wake up.

When Mom and Watson left, so did Charlie, but I tiptoed over to Emily's crib and looked down at her.

Hello, there, I thought. You are a very special little girl. I guess you are lucky, too. You found a family. And we are lucky. We found you. Do you know how much we want you? No? Well, you will when you're older, because we will tell you.

You have a lot of brothers, by the way. You have two sisters, as well. And a mom and a dad and a cat and a dog. Someday you'll know all this.

I tiptoed out of Emily's room — my new sister's room. Emily, I decided, was the best Mother's Day present ever.

About the Author

Ann M. Martin's The Baby-sitters Club has sold over 190 million copies and inspired a generation of young readers. Her novels include the Newbery Honor Book *A Corner of the Universe*, *A Dog's Life*, and the Main Street series. She lives in upstate New York.

Keep reading for a sneak peek at the next book from The Baby-sitters Club!

Mary Anne and the Search for Tigger

"Ti-i-i-igger! Ti-i-i-igger!" we called. We walked all around our yard. We shone the lights under bushes, up trees, in shrubbery. The longer we looked, the worse I felt. There was this awful feeling in the pit of my stomach, like I had swallowed a pebble and it had grown into a rock. Now it was growing into a boulder.

Dad must have seen me looking discouraged, because he said brightly, "I've got an idea," and ran inside. When he came out, he was carrying two of Tigger's toys. He gave me one, and we walked around the yard again, this time shaking the toys so that the balls jingled.

"Come play! Ti-i-i-igger, come play!"

No Tigger. (The rock had just about reached boulder proportions.)

"Dad!" I called, and he came running around the side of the house. "I don't think he's here. I really don't."

My father put his arm around my shoulders. "Maybe not. Maybe he's off on an adventure. Anyway, I don't think there's any point in looking for him outside now. It's too dark. Besides, if he were around here, he would have come to us by now."

I nodded. "I know."

"So let's go in."

Dad and I went into a house. A huge lump was forming in my throat. Maybe it was that boulder.

"I suggest we go on and make ourselves a nice dinner," my father said cheerfully. "If Tigger's off enjoying himself, then we might as well enjoy ourselves."

I looked at Tigger's bowl. The food was starting to congeal and the milk was turning brown. Tigger probably wouldn't eat it tonight. How sad.

Dad saw me looking at the dish and said, "When I was growing up, our next-door neighbors had a cat who disappeared at least once a week. He just liked to take trips."

"But Tigger is so little," I replied. I turned on the burner under the pot of water, while Dad began cutting up the tomatoes and cucumbers and celery and carrots for our salad. He didn't look worried. How come I felt so worried? Because I'm a worrywart, that's why.

We ate our dinner. Well, Dad ate his dinner. I tried to eat mine, but all I could get down were three mouthfuls of salad.

"Mary Anne," said my father, looking at my full plate, "what time is it?"

"Seven-thirty?" I answered. (Why was he asking? He was wearing his watch.)

"And when was the last time you saw Tigger?"

"Just before five-thirty."

"So he's only been missing for two hours," Dad pointed out. "He could be taking a nap somewhere, for all we know."

"He did have a pretty exciting afternoon," I said slowly. "Lots of visitors. And he does sleep soundly."

"I'll say," said Dad. "He could sleep through a tornado."

I felt cheered up. I felt so cheered up that I called Dawn and said, "You'll never guess what. Tigger is off taking a nap, and he's hidden himself so well that Dad and I can't find him!"

Dawn giggled. She likes Tigger stories. Then she said, "Okay, my turn. *You'll* never guess what. Our parents are going out again."

"They are? Dad didn't say anything."

"Well, it's no big deal. They're just going to a parents meeting at school together. But that's something, isn't it?"

"Sure," I replied. "That's something."

Dawn and I talked for the exact ten minutes that I'm allowed. Then we hung up. Then she called back. We talked for ten more minutes. That's one way of getting around Dad's telephone rule without actually breaking it.

After the second call, we hung up for good, though. I didn't want to press my luck. I watched some TV. I read two chapters in this really great book called *A Swiftly Tilting Planet*, by Madeleine L'Engle. I checked over my list of weekend homework assignments. And then I looked at my watch. Ten o'clock! Not only was it almost time to go to bed, but Tigger had been missing for four and a half hours.

I marched into my father's den, where he was doing some paperwork.

"Excuse me," I said, "but do you think Tigger has been taking a four-and-a-half hour nap?"

"Hmm?" Dad looked bleary-eyed.

"It's ten o'clock. Do you know where Tigger is?" I said.

Dad didn't get the joke, but he did look vaguely surprised. "Still missing, is he? Mary Anne, he'll turn up. He's just gone off on a jaunt. Cats do that, you know."

I wasn't convinced, but I went to bed anyway. I left my window open in case he turned up outside and began mewing. Then I lay down in bed. But I couldn't go to sleep. How could I sleep with Tigger missing? And he *was* missing, just like Dad had said.

He had disappeared.

At eleven-thirty, my father went to bed. I know because I was still awake. I knelt on my bed and looked out the window. I couldn't see anything, though. The sky was still overcast, so the clouds covered the moon.

I lay down again. At last I went to sleep. I woke up at one-thirty, thinking I heard mewing.

"Tigger? Tigger?" I called softly.

Nothing. I must have dreamed it.

The same thing happened at ten minutes past three, at 4:45, at 6:20, and at seven-thirty, when I finally decided to get up.

I ran down to the kitchen. "Is Tigger back?" I asked my father. He was sitting at the table with a cup of coffee and the newspaper.

This time he looked more worried than surprised. "No," said Dad. "He's not."

I sank into my chair. Now what?

Dad had fixed pancakes for breakfast and I tried to eat them, but I couldn't. Instead, I excused myself from the table, went to my room, got dressed, then went out to search the yard. The clouds were gone and the day was sunny and bright, but I couldn't find Tigger. I was glad there were no bodies in the road or under high trees, but . . . where *was* he?

All morning, I watched for Tigger and worried. When afternoon came, I realized I would have to leave for Logan's to baby-sit. It was the last thing I wanted to do. But Dad would be home. He could watch for Tigger. And with any luck, by the time I got back, Tigger would be back, too.

Want more baby-sitting?

THE BABY-SITTERS CLUB®

And many more!

Don't miss any of the books in the Baby-sitters Club series by Ann M. Martin—available as ebooks

DON'T MISS
THE BABY-SITTERS CLUB
GRAPHIC NOVELS!

KRISTY'S GREAT IDEA

THE TRUTH ABOUT STACEY

MARY ANNE SAVES THE DAY

CLAUDIA AND MEAN JANINE

DAWN AND THE IMPOSSIBLE THREE

KRISTY'S BIG DAY

BOY-CRAZY STACEY

LOGAN LIKES MARY ANNE!

CLAUDIA AND THE NEW GIRL

graphix

AN IMPRINT OF

SCHOLASTIC

scholastic.com/graphix

BSC